Praise for *Cooper and Packrat: Mystery on Pine Lake*

A Junior Library Guild Selection
2014 Maine State Book Award Finalist

"Mystery and adventure make this a suspenseful, can't-put-it-down book, but it's Cooper and Packrat's blind determination to save the loons against all odds that will steal your heart. I closed the book longing to hear that beautiful call only a loon can make." — Jo Knowles, author of *See You at Harry's*

"Packed with intrigue and sweet humor, this mystery with a conservation twist will grab young readers . . . Wight has penned a winning cast of characters, dialogue that sparkles and a plot that flies . . . A story that should turn even the most finicky readers into happy campers." — *Kirkus Reviews*

"Quirky characters and realistic dialogue will make this suspenseful eco-mystery a favorite summer read of any wildlife-lover." — *Foreword Reviews*

ISLANDPORT PRESS

COOPER AND PACKRAT

Mystery
on
Pine Lake

By Tamra Wight
Illustrations by Carl DiRocco

ISLANDPORT PRESS

ISLANDPORT PRESS
P. O. Box 10
Yarmouth, Maine 04096
www.islandportpress.com
books@islandportpress.com

ISBN: 978-1-939017-02-4
Library of Congress Control Number: 2013930186

Dean L. Lunt, Publisher
Front and back cover art: Carl DiRocco
Book jacket design: Karen Hoots / Hoots Design
Book design: Michelle Lunt / Islandport Press

For Red and Lois,
and Ron and Lee—
parents who are loved more than they know.

Chapter 1

Loons have been known to battle to the death to protect their territory, but the argument usually ends with the loser giving up and flying away.

Don't let it be a gross one, don't let it be a gross one, I prayed over and over in my head as I looked down on the metal trash can. Grasping the lid handle, I hoped this one would have the usual trash on top, like half-eaten burgers, slimy potato salad, plastic marshmallow bags, empty Hershey bar wrappers, or a squished-up graham cracker box.

I sucked in a breath and lifted the lid. Flies came out like a puff of steam. The lifeless, black beady eyes of some half-eaten lobsters lay on top of the trash, staring up at me. Little white maggots squiggled in and out of the leg holes. I groaned and let my breath out in a *whoosh*.

I quickly grabbed the bag with two hands and hauled it up and out of the can to set it on the ground. The lobster shells and guts shifted. Their horrible stench flew right up my nose.

Don't throw up, don't throw up, don't throw up. My throat started to do that watery thing, and I tried breathing really fast to get it to stop. Then I felt something in my mouth.

Something buzzing.

A fly!

I dropped the bag and leaned forward to spit on the ground again and again and again. Shuddering, I spit one more time to make sure there wasn't a wing or an antenna still floating around under my tongue or something. Then I rubbed my sleeve over my mouth as I quickly checked over both shoulders. Whew. It didn't look like anybody had seen my almost-hurl.

Taking a breath, I held it in deep this time, and double-knotted the bag as tightly as I could.

Why did I always get the ultra-gross trash cans?

On the other side of the road, Dad whistled as he walked from campsite to campsite, emptying cans. He'd already tied three bags to my one, grabbing them by the knot and heaving them high into the air to land on all the other bags in the dump truck bed. I had no idea what he had to whistle about. I mean, I could think of a gazillion things I'd rather be doing on a drizzly Saturday morning in May than almost barfing up a fly.

I searched the truck bed for the perfect landing spot so the bag wouldn't bounce back out or get hung up on the tall wooden sides. I swung it back and forth like a horseshoe. Just as I opened my hand to let the bag fly, my arm got bumped from behind.

I realized two things at the exact same time. One, it was no accidental bump. I knew this from the evil grin Roy shot me over his shoulder as he rode past on his bike. And two, that bag had gone straight up in the air over my head.

Ducking quickly out of the way, I then turned to watch helplessly as the bag hit the ground and split wide open like an old jack-o'-lantern that'd been heaved onto someone's driveway. Coffee grounds, potato peels, slimy green paper towels, little cereal boxes, and a carton of chunky milk exploded from it. Splatters of lobster guts hit my sneakers and the bottom of my jeans.

I glared at Roy, who'd skidded to a stop next to my dad to gloat over the mess.

"Cooper!" Dad yelled. "How many times have I told you to be more careful?"

"Roy hit my arm on purpose!"

Roy's smug smile turned to a sad little frown in the split second it took for Dad to look down at him. "Honest, Mr. Wilder, it was an accident. I was trying to go around the puddle. I didn't see Cooper there, doing the trash run."

Those last two words were said with just enough of a sneer for me to hear it, and my dad to miss it.

Dad put a hand on Roy's damp, red-haired head. "After all the rain we've had, I'm surprised you can avoid puddles at all." He looked at me. "How about you apologize to Roy?"

"But, Dad . . . he . . . he really . . ."

Roy's smug smile was back, now that Dad was looking my way. I balled up my hands, itching to charge that liar and knock him off his bike into one of the puddles he'd claimed to be avoiding.

I'd stomped halfway to the dump truck for a shovel and a rake before Dad cleared his throat. Rolling my eyes, I turned to give Roy a wicked sarcastic apology that would probably get me a speech from Dad. But before I could say a word, a voice came from behind me.

"The kid on the bike did it on purpose." A skinny boy about my age and size stepped up next to me. He and his mom had moved into site six yesterday, and he'd kind of stuck in my mind on account of the big tan trench coat he wore all the time.

Roy scowled at the new kid. "You're a big fat liar!"

The kid pushed his wet, brown, shaggy bangs to one side and stared coolly at Roy. "I saw you."

Dad held up both hands, looking between the two kids. "Ohhh-kay. I'm sure there's a good explanation here. Somewhere. Let's let it go for now. Coop and I need to get this trash run done so we can get to the dump before it starts raining again."

Dad went to get an empty trash bag. Roy looked at the new kid and me, raised his fist, and silently motioned it into the palm of his other hand before racing off on his bike toward the playground.

The new kid reached for my shovel to help. As I raked the trash into a pile for him to pick up, I said, "Thanks!"

"No problem." He was about to say more when we heard static. I put a hand to my camp radio, half expecting it to be Mom needing me to do a chore, or Molly wanting me to push her on the swing or something. But it wasn't my radio making all the noise. I looked at the new kid. He was elbow deep in one of the many outside pockets of his detective-like coat. Pulling out his own walkie-talkie, he sighed into it. "Mom?"

More static.

"Mom! Hold the button down, *then* talk."

Laughter came through. "I'll figure it out soon, Pete, I promise," she said. "Breakfast is ready. Come on back to the site."

"Waffles," he said, rubbing his stomach with a grin. "Catch up with you in a bit?"

I shook my head. "Maybe later? Dad and I are going out on the lake after the trash run." Feeling Dad's hand on my shoulder, I grinned up at him.

But he looked down at me with a sad I-hope-you'll-understand-when-I-ditch-you-again-to-work look.

"Dad! You promised you'd go this time. You said, 'No matter what'!"

"I know, I know. But something's come up. A camper on Raccoon Trail told your mom there's a dead tree behind his pop-up that's leaning heavy to one side this morning." Dad lifted his hat to run a hand through his short hair. "And of course, it's leaning toward the campsite. So before the wind and the rain drop it, I've got to chop the tree down, cut it up, and clean up the mess."

My words came out in a rush. "But patrolling the lake is important too! The loons haven't laid their eggs yet. They're wicked late. What if they don't lay any at all? You told me more and more campers were coming to see them, right? The eagle babies are poking their heads above the nest now, and the beavers have been—"

"Cooper, you're twelve now." Dad frowned. "You need to under-stand that just because we're the owners doesn't mean I can drop every-thing when I feel like it and play game warden with you."

"I don't *play* it, Dad—I do it! And I haven't *done it* in, like, a week. Please?"

Dad squeezed my shoulder, which was code for *Sorry, but no means no.*

I stepped out from under his hand. Without Dad, I couldn't go out on the lake. Rule of two: No fishing without a friend. No boating with-out a friend.

Only, I didn't have any friends right now. Or did I?

Ignoring the tight feeling in my throat, I called out to the new kid who was walking away.

"Hey!" What had his mom called him? "Umm, Pete?" When he turned around, I said, "Change in plans! Want to go out on the lake? In half an hour?"

Pete gave me a thumbs-up. "Get me when you're done. I'll hang out on the playground after I eat."

I breathed a sigh of relief. Now if I could just get this trash run done before one of the camp kids told him he wasn't supposed to hang out with me.

As Dad and I finished scooping up Roy's exploded mess, he tried talking to me, but yes and no answers were all he was getting. I'd been waiting days—no, a month—to go out in the canoe with him. No way was I forgiving him in two minutes.

The drizzle had stopped, but now the mayflies were out in full force. I slapped the back of my neck and rubbed my short, dirty-blond hair every time they swarmed me. Dad and I took care of the last can on the street, then he jumped in the truck's driver seat while I stood outside on the passenger side running board. Those mayflies couldn't land on me to suck my blood as long as we were rolling.

At the end of the road, Dad took a right. He was only driving about five miles an hour, but the wind made my eyes sting. Pines, maples, birches, and elms stood on both sides of the road as far as I could see. Sixty acres full of nature, and it was all ours. Wilder Family Campground.

One hand on the door handle, I reached out as far as I could to slap the heavy branches out of my way, so I didn't get swatted in the face or legs.

"Cooper!" Dad said, his sharp voice almost making me jump back off the running board. "Hold on with both hands. If you fall off and get hurt, your mother will never let us hear the end of it."

When we reached the lake, the trees opened up to show a large beach with a roped-off swimming area. To the left of that, paddle boards, kayaks, canoes, and rowboats in every size and color were tied to our docks. Back from the beach under the pine grove stood picnic tables and grills on posts.

Dad parked and I leaned in the open passenger window. "So, I'll do the beach cans, then go back up to get the game-room and playground cans," I said. "Then I'm done for the morning, right?"

"Yep. Let's meet at say, one o'clock, to clean the bathrooms."

I glanced at Dad's watch. Counting the cans I still had to empty, and a trip to the dump to help him unload, Pete and I would get about two hours to kayak. *I wonder if he likes to fish?*

As I jumped off the running board, a short, baldish, round guy wearing a green raincoat looked our way from where he stood on the dock. Arms waving in a big way, Mr. Beakman shouted, "Hey, Jim! Got a minute?" When Dad got out of the truck and nodded, the man said, "Just need to tie up my boat first."

I knew I was about to whine like Molly whenever she lost her purple stuffed elephant, but there was no stopping it. Forgetting how mad I was at him, I went back to tug Dad's sleeve and beg with everything I had. "C'mon, Dad! We don't have time to listen to Mr. Beakman complain again. The new kid's waiting, and I don't want him going off with someone else—"

"Cooper!" Dad's voice was firm, but there was a twinkle in his eye too. "His name is Mr. *Bakeman*. How many times do I have to tell you, making fun of his nose isn't nice! Talking to the campers, even the grumbly ones, is part of our job. It's called customer service."

When Mom and Dad bought the campground a couple of years ago and moved us from the city streets of Portland to the wooded edges of Pine Lake, I knew I'd love nature watching, hiking, and hanging with kids from all over the country. But there were three things I hadn't counted on. The first was chores, like cleaning bathrooms and emptying 132 trash cans twice a week. The second was sharing Mom and Dad with all the campers, all the time. And the third was customer service. It meant smiling, listening, and being nice to customers. And their kids. Even the mean ones.

Dad and I watched Mr. Beakman step off the dock and raise an arm toward us to tell us he was on his way over. Suddenly, his right leg buckled a little as he tripped over a tree root and wobbled before catching his balance again. Wiping the tip of his shiny white sneaker on the back of his other pant leg, he grumbled the whole time about how dirty the dirt was.

"I think," I said quietly, "I'd rather do trash pickup than customer service."

Chapter 2

Loons spend most of their life on the water, or under it. They're on land less than a day after they're born, and then again only to nest. Sometimes a loon is called a feathered fish.

Dad made a snarfing noise before covering it with a fake cough as a still-grumbling Mr. Beakman walked over to us.

"Hey, Al! How's the fishing been?" Dad said, holding out a hand to Mr. Beakman.

"Terrible—just terrible!" Mr. Beakman said, throwing an arm out toward the lake. "That's what I want to talk to you about."

The lake was as calm as could be, an eagle circling overhead.

"There I was," Mr. Beakman said, "sitting in the rain for hours, getting eaten alive by those monster mosquitoes of yours, and all I caught was a little four-inch bass. Then one of your loons had the nerve to pop up beside my boat with a seven-inch trout in its beak. Swallowed it whole right in front of me, too!"

Dad chuckled. "Now, Al, I'm sure—"

"They eat two pounds of food a day." Mr. Beakman held up two fingers, as if we didn't know what "two" was. "Each! Have you ever held four pounds of fish in your hands? Mark my words, they'll fish out your lake if you don't do something."

I shifted from one foot to the other, then back again. *Do something?* What'd he mean by that? I opened my mouth to tell him to go jump in the lake. But then Dad folded his arms.

If Mr. Beakman knew Dad like I know Dad, he'd realized that he'd gone too far.

"There's nothing to be done," Dad said firmly. "Loons are one of the things our campers come to see. They've been nesting on the lake longer than my family's owned the campground, and they haven't fished it out yet." Dad put a hand on my shoulder. "Cooper here, he's our loon expert. Did a school report on them in fifth grade last year. Cooper, tell Mr. Bakeman what else the loons eat besides fish."

I sighed. It was an eagle report, and it was two years ago when I was in the fourth grade, but I knew what Dad was looking for. "They eat frogs, crayfish, and leeches too."

Mr. Beakman rolled his eyes. "Tell that to the loon who ate my trout."

Ha! He's just jealous because the loons fish better than he does—and have smaller beaks, too.

While Dad distracted Mr. Beakman by changing the subject and asking what kind of bait he was using, I wandered onto the end of the dock. Out toward the middle of the lake was a long, skinny island. At about three hundred feet long and forty feet wide, it wasn't big enough for people to live on, but that made it perfect for loons. They always nested on the opposite side from what I could see from our beach. I'd been trying desperately to kayak out there for days, but with all the rain and chores and homework, I hadn't had much luck. Were they just late laying their eggs this year? Or had they already laid them, and lost them to some animal?

Like it knew I'd been thinking about it, one of the loons silently popped out of the water a few feet away. Sometimes campers call them cormorants or ducks by mistake. I suppose I would too, if I only saw its black-and-white-checkered body, white belly, black head, and long, sharp black beak. But it was the white block necklace around its neck and its red eyes—good for seeing underwater—that told me it was a loon.

I cupped my hands around my mouth and called out with the soft loon hoots I'd been practicing. The loon quickly looked my way, then dived under the water as quietly as it had appeared. Ripples in the water were the only proof it'd been there.

So much for making contact with loons. There was still the new camper, though.

Dad gave me the nod to go ahead, so I pulled the bags from the lake cans, threw them on the truck, and started walking back up the way we'd come. Dad would catch up. It might be two minutes, or twenty-two minutes, with a "Sorry, Coop, but so-and-so asked me to do blah-blah-blah for them," but he'd follow.

Thinking about finally getting out in the kayak to check on the loons, I started walking a little faster. I was still mad at Dad 'cause he wouldn't go, but it'd be really cool to kayak with a friend.

The trash can outside the game room was full of junk food wrappers and soda bottles. I had pulled the bag and tied it when I overheard a group of kids going by.

"You have to see this!"

"Roy's gonna—"

The words faded out as the kids jogged past me toward the playground, so I couldn't hear the end of the sentence, but it wasn't a good sign.

I left the bag next to the can and walked around the corner of the game room. There was a growing circle of kids on the playground. It wasn't a let's-all-hang-out-and-play-together-nicely circle, either. More like a there's-gonna-be-a-fight circle.

In the middle was Roy, with his finger pointed at Pete's chest.

"I asked you, what's up with the stupid coat?!"

Why was I not surprised? Any kid who was a friend of mine automatically made Roy's "must bully" list.

Pete said, "What's it to you?"

Roy narrowed his eyes. He lowered his brows. When Pete didn't blink, Roy turned to the crowd. "I bet he found that coat in a dumpster. Maybe he stole it from some homeless guy."

A couple of kids snickered. The rest shuffled their feet and looked as if they wanted to be somewhere else, like on the other side of the campground, or across the lake. They couldn't leave, though. That would put *them* on Roy's list.

Pete squared his shoulders. "All my stuff's in this coat."

Roy sneered. "All of it? Can't be much."

Pete shrugged. "I don't need much to camp."

Roy laughed as his eyes scanned the crowd. A few kids laughed with him. Roy turned back to the kid. "Make you a deal. I'll name something I bring to camp all the time. If you have it in there," he flicked the collar of Pete's coat, "I'll leave you alone."

I caught Pete's eye and shook my head slightly. Roy never played fair.

"Okay," said Pete. "I'll take your bet."

"And what'll *you* do if you don't have it?" Roy asked.

Pete smiled. "I'll eat my coat."

There was a lot of murmuring in the circle. Even though I thought my new friend was doomed, I had to bite my tongue to keep from snickering at the confused look on Roy's face when he repeated, "You'll . . . *eat* it?"

Pete nodded.

Roy took a step back. I swear I saw question marks floating over his head. "I can guess anything?" he asked.

"Anything you can prove you have here when you're camping."

Slowly, a grin spread across Roy's face. "Okay. You're on."

Roy walked back and forth. Every now and then he'd stop, look like he was going to say something, then smile again and start pacing. I had to give Pete credit. He stood stone-still, watching Roy with serious eyes.

Roy might not have been freaking him out, but he was freaking *me* out! I'd only met Pete for a minute, but I wanted him to win this bet in the worst way.

Finally, Roy stopped pacing. He locked eyes with the kid. "I," he said, pausing to wink at the crowd, "brought a telescope from home."

That made me as mad as a hornet that'd just been swatted.

"As if!" I yelled. The crowd parted as I stormed over to Pete. "He has no telescope. Make him choose something else."

Roy snorted. "You have no idea what I have."

I got nose to nose with the pain-in-my-butt. "You were *never* into that kind of stuff."

"Three years is a long time, Nature Boy. Maybe I'm into it n—"

A gasp from the crowd made Roy and me turn toward Pete. He was holding open one side of his coat while digging, elbow deep, into a long, skinny, inside pocket. When his hand stopped moving, he locked eyes with Roy and smiled. Ever so slowly, he pulled out a long black tube. The crowd moved closer as he twisted off the cover and turned it upside down.

A two-foot-long silver thing slid into his hand.

No way! I wasn't sure if I'd said the words out loud, but I figured I must have when Pete looked at me and grinned. In three quick moves, he unfolded the silver thing into a tabletop telescope on three legs, and stood it on the picnic table behind him.

"Ta-da!" he said.

I heard a couple of quiet *Yeah*s from the back of the crowd. There were even some louder *Wow*s. Roy snapped his mouth shut and straightened his shoulders. Nodding to his buddies to follow, he stormed away to the game room.

Chapter 3

Maine loons usually lay their eggs from mid-May to mid-June.

"Pete! That was awesome!" I said. "The way you played Roy like that. How'd you do it? Are you a magician?"

"Nah," he said, folding up the telescope to put it back into its case. "I just like gadgets and stuff. By the way, only my mom and grandma call me Pete. My friends back home in Weld call me Packrat." He opened one side of his coat to slide the case back into its inside pocket.

"I'm Cooper. Wilder. But you probably guessed that."

He smiled. "Yeah, the trash-run job kind of gave it away."

Packrat hung around with me while I waited for Dad to catch up with the dump truck so we could take the load of trash to the dump. I'd found some crunched-up soda case boxes and we sat on them on top of the picnic table so we wouldn't get our butts wet. Feet resting on the benches, I pounded him with questions.

"How long are you here for?"

"We're seasonal. Mom bought the camper on site six so we could be closer to my grandma. She broke her hip a couple of weeks ago, and we were driving back and forth, an hour and a half each way, to see her. Now she's only ten minutes down the road."

"You're out of school already?"

"I wish! We're just weekenders now. When school gets out, Mom says we'll move down here for the whole summer. Then when school starts again in the fall, we'll go back to only coming down on weekends."

I opened my mouth to ask another question, but Packrat beat me to it. "So what's Roy's story?"

"We used to be friends when I lived in Portland, before my parents bought this place and moved us here." I was picking apart a pinecone, throwing the scales on the ground one by one. "I didn't see him for a year, until his family became seasonal campers. But I don't know . . . he was different. I just wanted to spend every day hiking the campground trails and kayaking the lake. He wanted to ride mountain bikes down the trails and race from one end of the lake to the other in his motor-boat. I mean, you can't see or hear or watch anything when you're flying around like that. Then there was this big thing—an argument, kind of. He stopped hanging with me, and started calling me Nature Boy."

"Are you?" Packrat asked.

I stiffened, turning to look at him. He wasn't laughing at me, though. He was dead serious.

I relaxed. "Kind of."

"Cool."

I heard Dad's truck before I saw it. Jumping off the picnic table, I grabbed the last of the trash bags and threw them on before he hit the brakes. Dad leaned out the window.

"Sorry about that, buddy. Mr. Bakeman had a lot of grumbling to do today."

Packrat spoke up. "Bakeman? The guy camped next to me?"

"Yeah," I said. "Watch out for him. Mr. *Beakman* doesn't like the dirt on his site. It's too shaded. His water hookup is in the wrong spot. Stuff like that."

Packrat snickered. "Beakman. Good one. He yelled out his window at the ravens this morning, 'cause they woke him up."

Two things made me realize that I'd be hanging with Packrat this summer. One, he knew the difference between a raven and a crow. Two, he understood how I felt about Beakman.

Dad tipped his head to one side and gave us an I-know-you're-right-but-it's-not-nice-to-make-fun-of-others look.

I figured I'd better introduce Packrat fast, before Dad gave me the customer service speech in front of my new friend. As I did, Packrat stuck out his hand to Dad.

Dad put his hands in the air. "Oh no, you don't want to do that. I've been handling bags of smelly, nasty tra—"

Dad's voice trailed off because Packrat had opened his coat to put his hand in a small inside pocket. Taking out a little bottle of hand sanitizer, he offered it to my father.

"Uhh . . . thanks." Dad held out a hand and Packrat pumped some of the clear liquid onto it.

"Mom makes me carry it," he said, dropping the bottle back into his pocket.

Dad pointed his thumb toward the bed of the truck. "How about I take this load to the dump myself? Then you'll have time to check on your loons before you have to eat lunch and do the one o'clock bathroom check."

"Really?" I asked.

"Really," he said.

I looked at Packrat and raised my eyebrows.

"I just have to get my life jacket," he said.

We hadn't even taken two steps when Dad called out, "Cooper! Turn your radio on."

"It *is* on!"

"Now turn it all the way up." Dad pointed his thumb upward. "In case Mom needs you."

I sighed, turning the knob as far as it would go. "Okay, okay. It's on and up. Can I go now?"

Dad just chuckled as he put the truck in gear. Packrat and I watched the dump truck roll away. It swayed from side to side on the dirt road, bags of trash threatening to fall over the tall wooden sides.

We walked toward Packrat's site, but he kept looking back over his shoulder at the truck. "I swear I'll never complain again about taking out our trash. You get an allowance for that?"

I shrugged. "Sort of. I keep bugging them for a real paycheck, though, you know? I want to get paid by the hour so I can get some good binoculars. And I want to make an emergency kit for when I patrol the lake. But my parents keep telling me I'm family. We all have to pitch in."

Once Dad's truck was out of sight, I turned the radio knob down. Mom always called right when I was in the middle of doing some of my favorite things. Like when I was out in the middle of the lake, reeling in a fish. Or watching a mother deer with her fawn. Or when I was the last person still hiding in Manhunt. I didn't want her calling me now to unplug a toilet in the ladies' bathroom. Not when I'd just started hanging with Packrat.

The two of us walked onto his site. He headed straight for an outside compartment next to the camper door. Just as he pulled out a life jacket, there was a very faint rumble of thunder.

We were kind of standing there, looking at each other, neither one wanting to make the call whether we stayed or went, when *crash!* A camper door slammed shut on the site behind Packrat's. Heavy footsteps started pacing across a wooden deck.

Packrat and I jumped, then froze when we heard Mr. Beakman's voice. "That's enough, Samantha! I'm not a child! I'm fine! Stop worrying." There was a long pause, then a big sigh. "Yes. I'm enjoying the lake. Getting a lot of fishing in, in spite of this blasted rain and those annoying loons."

Packrat pointed to his camper door, then tiptoed toward it. Once inside, we silently moved toward the windows facing Mr. Beakman's site, careful to stay behind the curtains. Packrat slowly turned the knob to flip the window open the tiniest bit.

Whatever the person on the cell phone was saying had Mr. Beakman pulling it away from his ear and frowning at it, before he put it back to listen. His face got all relaxed and almost, well, happy. "I know, I know . . . no, I'll stay here. It's a pretty campground; quiet, too. The owners are nice, even if they don't understand what a menace those loons are." He paused a moment to listen to the person on the other end. "Well, there's not just two of them now, either. They've gone and laid eggs."

I gasped, then clamped a hand over my mouth. *Eggs!* The loons had laid their eggs! Yes! That was good news.

Mr. Beakman started pacing again. "They'd make a better omelet, as far as I'm concerned."

That was bad news.

"Look, Samantha, sweetheart, I've got to go. I was heading down to my boat when you called. I need to take care of something—two somethings, actually . . . Yes, of course I'll catch one for you." Mr. Beakman chuckled as he opened the door to his truck and climbed in. "Talk to you later. Bye."

I looked at Packrat. "We have to follow him! I think he's gonna hurt the loon eggs!"

Chapter 4

Loons call out with a soft hoot *to find, and check in with, their family members.*

Our feet pounded the dirt as we took off down the main road. While we'd been in the camper, the wind had picked up a little, and the sky was spitting big fat raindrops. I could hear Packrat breathing heavily, his coat flapping as his arms pumped up and down. Our feet slapped the ground in time with one another. Rounding the corner, we saw Mr. Beakman's truck way ahead, making the turn that would take him down to the lake.

I made my move and sped up a little, but had to come to a screeching stop when Mom rushed out of the campground office to stand in my path. Camp radio in her hand, she flagged me down. "Cooper? I've been calling you for the past ten minutes!"

I threw back my head and groaned. "Moooooom! C'mon! I have to go out on the lake!"

Either Mom didn't hear me, or she was ignoring me. Pointing with the radio toward two huge motor homes pulling through the gate, she said, "I have to check these campers in, but I can't see Molly on the playground. Go make sure she's still there, please?"

"Where's Dad?"

"He took the trash to the dump."

Duh. I'd forgotten. "C'mon, Mom. The little pest's probably just hiding from the thunder, under the climber."

"Cooo-per." Mom's voice held a hint of warning.

No, no, no! This couldn't be happening now! "Mom, please." I tried to keep my voice calm. "It's an emergency. I think Mr. Beakman's gonna hurt the loon eggs."

Mom stared at me blankly for a minute. "Beakman? You mean Mr. Bakeman? Cooper!" She shook her head. "I know he's a grumbler, but I'm sure he wouldn't do anything like *that*." She pointed her radio at me. "Your sister is missing."

Thunder rolled long and loud overhead, as if someone up there were warning me to listen to her, or else.

"Yeah, yeah," I said, too embarrassed at being yelled at by my mom to look Packrat's way. "I got it. Find the shrimp."

I jogged to the playground and over to the climber, Packrat right behind me. I figured it'd only take a minute because Molly hid in the exact same place every time. There was a half-door and some walls underneath the big twirly slide which acted as a hidden fort for little kids. Molly liked to climb in there when she was sad or mad. Or scared.

As I got closer, I heard girly giggling from behind the door. I winked at Packrat, then growled, "Little girl, little girl, let me come in! *Rrrrrrrrroooaaaarrr!*" Then I threw the door open wide. Two little girls screamed back at me at the top of their lungs, pressing themselves as far back in the little room as they could go.

Neither one was Molly.

After saying "Sorry" to them and their angry mothers forty times, I was finally forgiven. Packrat handing out lollipops from one of his pockets didn't hurt either. The girls told us they'd seen Molly a little while ago, but not in the last couple of minutes.

She wasn't at the top of the climber. No one on the playground had seen her. Nor had anyone in the game room. I checked the pool area just in case, but I knew she wouldn't be there because she hadn't learned to swim yet, and it was against the rules for her to be inside the pool fence without Mom or Dad. Then again, it was against the rules for her to leave the playground, too.

I'd just finished checking the house and was running back to Mom with the bad news when she came out of the office. "Cooper?"

"Mom!" I put my hands on my knees and doubled over. Between gasps for air, I said, "I can't . . . find her . . . anywhere!"

Mom started listing off all the usual places, and I saw her face fall each time I said, "Checked it!"

She locked the front door to the store. The phone rang. She ignored it. That was a first.

"What now?" I asked.

"Start calling her, Cooper. Really loudly!"

I hollered as I walked toward the playground. "Moooo-lllllllllllyyy! Hey, Shrimp! Where are you!" Packrat jogged to the other side by the rec hall and started calling there. Mom's voice echoed back from over by the house. I could hear it crack with worry from here.

My hands balled into fists. I got angrier and angrier every time I called her name. In my mind, I saw Beakman's boat pulling up near the loon nest and him bashing the eggs with a paddle over and over again while the loons wailed helplessly just offshore. But could I do anything about it? No! Because Molly had to go and hide from the thunder, and Mom wouldn't listen to me about Beakman.

Okay, okay, I have to admit that I was starting to get a little worried about Molly too. She'd never gone outside the boundaries Mom set for her. Since she was only four, the playground, the game room, and the house were the only places she could go without us, and they were all bunched together right behind the campground office and store. Break that rule to go out into the campsites and it meant being grounded for a whole day, sitting in Mom's camp office with no TV, no computer, and no handheld electronics of any kind. To Molly, that would be like me getting grounded from the lake and the loons.

I could only think of two reasons why she wasn't answering us. One, she was hurt and couldn't answer. Or two, someone wouldn't let her.

I jogged off the playground toward the main road. "Mollll-yyy! Molly! Answer us!"

"Here I am, Cooper."

I turned quickly, ready to give her a really big piece of my mind for scaring me. Instead, I froze when I saw Beakman holding her hand, walking toward us from his campsite.

But how? Wasn't he . . .

"Did you lose something?" he barked at me.

I couldn't think. Molly and Beakman? "She was supposed to be—I mean, Mom said . . ." Mr. Beakman's eyes practically burned holes through mine as he stared at me. The corners of his mouth were turned so far downward, he looked like bulldog.

I took a step back. Why was he mad at me?

Luckily, Mom came running up. She stopped for a second when she saw Mr. Beakman with Molly. Then she fell to her knees and grabbed her, saying "Oh, Molly!" Pushing Molly back to arm's length, she began the yelling. "Where were you?"

Molly smiled up at the man who'd brought her back. "I got scared of the thunder, and there were some girls in my fort. So I went to the next fort. Mr. Bakeman has a granddaughter my age. Her name is Mia."

I almost fell over when Beakman looked down at Molly with an aren't-you-the-cutest-thing look.

Mom stood up to shake Mr. Beakman's hand. Her smile wavered a little, as she said, "Thank . . . thank you."

I could tell Mom's tears were right behind her eyelids, ready to flow like a waterfall. I guess Mr. Beakman could tell, too, because he took her hand in both of his. "Not a problem, Joan. These things happen. I found her on my screen room floor, playing with her stuffed elephant. I didn't even have a chance to ask her where her campsite was, when you all started calling and I put two and two together."

"But," I said, looking from Mr. Beakman to Molly and back again, "we were just there. You went to the lake to take care of two some-things, and," I pointed to Molly, "you weren't in his screen room."

Mr. Beakman slowly turned to look at Packrat and me. "How'd you know I was going to bail my boat?"

Thunder cracked overhead.

My first thought was: *Bail his boat? Whew.*

My second thought was: *Uh-oh.*

Packrat shuffled from one foot to another and stammered, "We were outside on my site. You were outside . . . on yours . . ."

Mr. Beakman frowned. "So you listened in on my phone call with my daughter instead of watching Mia . . . Molly. I mean Molly."

Packrat and I exchanged a quick look.

"Not on purpose," I said.

"Just the end," Packrat fibbed. "Right before you drove away."

"Good thing I came back for my hat," Beakman growled. "How could you lose her like that?"

"Oh no," Mom said, looking from Mr. Beakman to Packrat and me, and then back to Mr. Beakman with a confused look. "*I* lost Molly. Me. One second she was playing on the climber, right outside the store win-dow. I turned to sell a couple of ice creams, looked back, and she was gone." Mom frowned at Molly. "Really! We've talked about this! It's very dangerous to go onto strangers' campsites . . ."

I tuned Mom out. I knew the routine from here. She'd tell Molly she was grounded, then she'd make her apologize to me and Mr. Beak-man. Then she'd say they were going to have a very, very long talk. And Molly would look up at her with her big blue eyes and promise never to do it again. Until next time.

When more thunder cracked overhead, Molly's skipping toward the store turned into a race, with Mom close behind. Mr. Beakman was fast-walking back to his camper, hands in his pockets, head down from the fat drops of rain that had begun to fall. Halfway to his site he looked back to shoot us one more narrow-eyed I'm-watching-you look.

No way was Mom gonna let me go out on the lake with a storm coming, but it helped to know that Mr. Beakman probably couldn't go out either.

Suddenly, I realized I wasn't getting wet. As Packrat held an umbrella over our heads, I decided he was going to be one cool friend to have.

"You thinking what I'm thinking?" he said.

I turned my gaze on Mr. Beakman's back. "Only if you're thinking that bailing out the boat was one something, not two."

Chapter 5

Some scientists believe loons have been on Earth for twenty million years.

Now that I knew the loons had laid their eggs, I was itching to do a lake patrol and see them for myself. No way could I get Mom to agree while it was thundering, though.

Packrat challenged me to a game of pool. I raced him to the game room and beat him by a foot, but I didn't get to gloat for long. Right away, he reached elbow deep into a long, skinny inside coat pocket to pull out two pieces of a pool stick. I thought it was broken or something, until he screwed them together. I'd been hustled.

He ended up winning, of course.

It was still spitting rain at lunchtime, but at least the thunder had stopped. We gobbled down a hot dog and fries at the Snack Shack before his mom called him back to his camper and my dad called to see if I was ready to do the bathroom cleaning with him yet.

Could anyone ever be ready to clean bathrooms?

"I'm finishing lunch, Dad." I dunked my last french fry in the ketchup on my plate.

"You didn't eat at the Snack Shack again, did you?"

I looked guiltily at Big Joe behind the counter. He shot me an if-he-asks-if-I-gave-you-that-lunch-I-didn't look.

"Umm . . . maybe?" I said.

Dad sighed loudly over the radio. "Your mom buys good food every week, Cooper. You could come home and make a sandwich once in a while instead of eating all the profits."

"I didn't *have* time to make lunch, Dad. I spent most of my time off looking for Molly. Then I played one fast game of pool with Packrat."

"Big Joe?" Dad's voice came over the radio. "You hear me tell my son to eat at home?"

I held the radio up to Big Joe. Holding down the button so he could answer, I mouthed the word *Sorry*.

Big Joe shook his head, then talked to the radio. "I heard you, Jim. But it's kind of been a slow day. If it wasn't for Cooper and his friend, I'd have had no customers."

Looking at the line of kids buying pizza slices, I smiled a *thank-you* to Big Joe.

Dad answered, "Tomorrow, Cooper, you eat at home. You can't live on hot dogs and french fries, you know."

Big Joe held up a burger and onion rings.

I choked back a laugh while answering Dad. "C'mon! You guys haven't come in for lunch since we opened this year. I hate eating alone."

"Then bring Molly or Packrat. End of discussion."

I sighed, grabbed my lunch stuff, and walked it to the trash can. "Okay, fine. I'm done eating now. I'll meet you in five, okay? Then I'm gonna go out in the kayak and see the loons."

This time it was Mom's voice on the radio. "Cooper, no boating today, okay? There are thunderstorm warnings until six o'clock. There's even a tornado warning the next county over."

"But Mom—the loon eggs!"

Dad came back on. "They've been having babies for hundreds of years, Cooper. I'm sure they know what to do."

"Millions of years," I shot back, before turning the radio off. Was I ever gonna get out on the lake this weekend?

As I walked toward the bathrooms, I heard Packrat's voice. "Hey, Mom, stop a sec!" His mom pulled up beside me in their car. Packrat leaned over to introduce us. After she told me how much she liked the campground and my parents, Packrat said, "We're going to my grand-ma's to make her supper. Want to hang out when I get back?"

That gave me a great idea. "Hey, I know it's still raining, but do you want to camp out in my tent on my front lawn tonight?"

"Yeah!" Packrat grinned. "I'll bring my sleeping bag."

An hour later, I burst out laughing, wondering which pocket he kept it in.

Chapter 6

When they feel threatened, loons can squeeze the
air out from between their feathers and from their
air sacs to sink silently below the surface of the water,
like a submarine.

After the game room had closed for the night at ten o'clock and all the kids had gone back to their campsites, Packrat and I slipped into the tent on my front lawn. I'd always wanted to camp out on my own campsite somewhere out in the middle of the campground, but Mom and Dad told me those were for the paying customers.

I'd argued that hauling trash and cleaning bathrooms should earn me one.

They'd just laughed. Then they'd told all their friends at one of their weekend campfires how clever I was, trying to work for my campsite. There were still a few adults who teased me by saying stuff like, "So, trying to get your own place, huh?," or "You don't have your eye on *my* site, do you?"

It was so humiliating.

After telling Packrat all of this, I added, "And that's what they do when I'm trying to learn how to be a game warden. They pat me on the head, tell me how cute I am, and walk away!"

Packrat unrolled his sleeping bag and plopped onto it, sitting cross-legged.

"Does everybody do that?"

"Game Warden Kate is really cool. I e-mail her when I see stuff on my patrols and she tells me what to look for. Tom—he's a neighbor at the other end of the lake—he does this once-a-week TV spot on the local station. He calls it *Community Connections,* and he tapes interesting stuff that's happening around here. He and I share notes about what we see on the lake too." I threw my hands in the air. "I just don't get why Mom and Dad don't care anymore, 'cause they used to take Molly and me canoeing and hiking all the time before we bought this place. It was our thing, you know? And it doesn't help that they won't let me go out by myself."

Packrat looked thoughtful. "None of the camp kids want to go?"

I shook my head and looked down at the flashlight I was twirling on the tent floor, hoping he wouldn't ask why.

"What do you do on a patrol?" he asked.

"I check for injured animals. Make lists of what I see for wildlife, and how many of each are on the lake. You know, like how many wood ducks I see in an hour. Or if the eagle babies have hatched. That kind of stuff."

"I'd go. That sounds cool." Packrat opened the left side of his coat. "So, what do you want to do? I have Uno, Skip-Bo, regular cards, poker chips, Mille Bornes . . ."

"How about Monopoly?" I asked, just to be a smart guy.

While crickets chirped all around us and tree frogs croaked, Packrat closed his coat. It was on the tip of my tongue to say, "Ha! I found something you don't have," when he opened the right side of his coat and pulled out a twelve-inch-square box. Across the cover were the words TRAVEL MONOPOLY.

We both fell over laughing. "Jerk!" I teased. "I thought I had you that time."

"Shhhhhhhhhh!" Mom's voice came from the window above us. "You'll wake your father. And it's quiet hours now."

I apologized to Packrat with a look. What kid wants to be quiet at ten o'clock when they're camping out with friends? I mean, really? It's one of the stupidest rules we have.

Packrat had already opened the box and unfolded the game board. "I'm the shoe," he said. I was leaning over the board, looking for the dog piece, when I heard shushing and muffled giggling.

Packrat and I shared a look. "I thought all kids were supposed to be on their sites?" he whispered.

"They are." Above our heads, the rumble of Dad's snoring drifted out a bedroom window. The lights were out, so I knew Mom had gone to bed too.

"Let's go see what's up." I nodded toward the giggles on the playground.

Packrat shut off his flashlight and put it away. We quietly pulled down the zipper on the tent door flap and snuck out. When our eyes had gotten used to the sudden darkness, we crossed the street and slipped behind the office, sneaking toward the playground the back way.

A breeze blew lightly, and the black shadowed trees danced, plopping leftover cold raindrops on our heads. Together we tiptoed into a small bunch of trees between us and the playground. Careful not to step on any twigs or leaves that might crunch and give us away, we slid from tree to tree until we saw groups of shadows running around the playground equipment.

Something dark swooped over our heads as we crouched low. Packrat ducked. Then he ducked again. "What are they doing?" he whispered. "Flying planes at night?"

I started to answer, but listened instead when I heard Roy's voice over all the other kids. "No! Not that way." We heard a frustrated groan, then, "Look. Don't throw them like a baseball. If you toss the net straight up, it'll open like a parachute on the way down."

I muttered, "Jerk. Messing with the bats that way."

"Bats? BATS!" Packrat jumped up, running his hands through his hair.

I made a grab for Packrat's trench coat and pulled him back down beside me. But it was too late.

Roy jogged over, half-growling, half-whispering, "What are *you* doin' here?"

I stood up. "We heard you at my house! If I can hear you, someone else will too!"

Roy cupped a hand behind his ear. All that could be heard from the closest campsites was snoring. I swear I heard my father's above the rest. Hopefully, Roy didn't know one *snnnnarrrkkkkk-nrrrkkkkk* from another.

"I'm not stupid. I staked it out first," he said proudly. "There's a couple campfires down on the lower road, but everybody on the main road's in bed. Besides, I went by your place first. Your father's snoring like a bear."

Darn it. He knew.

"Bats?" Packrat ducked again as another swooped us.

"They're only brown bats," I muttered, still a little annoyed he'd gotten us caught. "All they do is eat mosquitoes. Three thousand a night."

Roy snickered. "Yeah. Nature Boy here put up houses for them. A dozen of them."

"You're not getting eaten alive, are you?" I shot back.

"Mosquitoes?" Packrat had lowered his arms to carefully look upward. Squinting into the darkness, he said, "Not blood?"

"Not blood."

"Cool. Okay. That's cool."

Roy laughed and flicked the collar on Packrat's coat. "What? You don't have any bat spray in one of your pockets?"

"Knock it off, Roy," I said.

"Or what?" he said, throwing his hand out toward the group of kids on the playground. "You'll rat on us like you ratted on me last time?"

I felt Packrat's eyes on me and was glad the dark hid how red I knew my face was. I should've known Roy would jump at the chance to tell my new friend.

With clenched fists, I took a step forward. Roy grinned and put both hands in the air. "Take it easy, Nature Boy. We're just studying the bats."

"Trapping them with a net isn't how you do it!"

A couple kids shushed us from across the playground. More than half had disappeared already, and the four or five left were grouped in the shadows. Roy glared at me. Lowering his voice, he said, "Great. You're scaring everybody away. Go home. Forget you saw anything. Then you won't have to tell on us when your mommy and daddy ask about it."

He jogged back to the group and started whispering to them, waving his hands around and sometimes pointing at me. I knew he was trying to convince them to stay. Some of the kids glanced my way; a couple shook their heads and backed off the playground.

Suddenly, we heard a familiar grumpy voice come from the darkness.

"What are you kids doing out here?"

In a flash Roy and his friends slipped deeper into the shadows. Even the bats made themselves scarce.

So guess who got caught in Mr. Beakman's flashlight beam?

Chapter 7

A loon's bill is approximately three inches long and can clamp tightly around its prey.

I held up a hand, shielding my eyes from Mr. Beakman's flashlight. His light was so strong, it felt like it was frying my brain and trying to come out my ears.

"Well?" Mr. Beakman barked. "I asked you a question, young man. What are you doing out after quiet hours?"

"We heard kids," I said, "messing with the bats." I bent over to pick up a piece of netting to show him. "They were throwing these up in the air and trying to catch them."

Packrat looked at me sharply.

Beakman looked creepier than usual, thanks to the flashlight beam. His eye sockets were pitch-black, his cheekbones looked like he hadn't eaten in weeks, and the rest of his face was grayish. Only the side of his nose was lit up.

"Who'd you catch?" he said, looking around.

"No one," I fibbed. "They were gone when we got here."

Over Mr. Beakman's shoulder, I saw the kids slipping from tree shadow to tree shadow, as they silently made their way off the playground. Except for Roy. He stood still in the shadow of the climber.

"Suuuuuure," Mr. Beakman dragged out that one word in such a way that I knew he didn't believe me. "Where's your father, anyway?"

"He did the security rounds already. He's home." I took a couple of steps backward, hoping he'd let us go and not march me to my front door to wake up my parents. I was positive that was exactly what Roy was waiting for. "We were heading back to tell him when you came."

"Yeah, yeah. Go on." He waved the flashlight toward my house. "Get out of here. Don't you be waking me up again, you hear?"

Packrat and I practically ran back to my front yard. As we tumbled into the tent, we started giggling quietly. I pointed up, to remind him Mom was probably listening.

We lay back on our sleeping bags. I put my hands behind my head.

Packrat said, "For a minute there, I thought you were gonna rat Roy out. That was pretty slick, the way you told the truth, but kind of lied too."

We were quiet for a minute. Then he blurted, "What'd he mean? You know, when Roy said you'd ratted him out before?"

I hesitated. It wasn't my proudest moment, having tattled on another kid. And it'd cost me too. "It was a couple years ago. He was sneaking out of his tent after his parents went to sleep in their camper."

"To hang out? Like tonight?"

"Nah. Worse. One night, his mom woke up and found him missing. She freaked out. Pounded on our front door to get Dad. He came in and woke me up to ask questions. And when he found out I'd known all along what Roy'd been doing at night, I got a lecture about how we're owners, and we had a responsibility to keep the campers safe, blah, blah, blah."

Packrat sucked in a breath. "Uh-oh . . . the guilt card. So what was he doing?"

"Hornpouting. Night-fishing in his boat."

"So fishing at night is bad?"

"Fishing for hornpout is fun!" I said. "But he didn't tell his mom where he was going, and she doesn't let him go out on the lake at night alone."

Woou-ou-ou-ou. Woou-ou-ou-ou.

Packrat sat straight up and grabbed his flashlight when he heard the fast, wavering call coming in off the lake. "What was *that?*"

I laughed. "Loons. You've never heard one before?"

Packrat shook his head. "Not like that! The ones I've heard made a long, slow, haunted-house kind of call. That sounded like a crazy lady laughing."

"There's two of them."

We listened as they called back and forth a few more times. Packrat rolled up his coat and put it under his head, lying back down.

Woou-ou-ou-ou.

"Tremolo call," I said firmly. Tipping my head, I listened some more. "It means they're all weirded out about something. Something's going on out there."

Packrat put both arms behind his head. "You pull nature facts out of your brain like I pull stuff out of my coat."

Hearing the loons cry back and forth again, I frowned. "Hey Pack-rat, want to go kayaking in the morning?"

Chapter 8

Loons may fly to a different lake to find food. They need about a quarter-mile of open water to take off, and can fly approximately 85 miles an hour.

At six in the morning, Packrat's battery-operated alarm clock started buzzing. *Bzzzzzzz. Bzzzzzzz. Bzzzzzzz.* Opening one eye, I grabbed for it, rolling it over and over in my hands until I found the off button.

Yawning, I stretched my arms up over my head. I couldn't help but shiver as they slid from the toasty-warm sleeping bag into the cool dawn air. I looked over at Packrat. At least, I hoped the lump at the bottom of his sleeping bag was him and not a skunk or something.

"Hey?" I nudged the lump. "Still want to go out in the kayak?"

I heard a snort and saw a twitch.

I took that as a Yes.

"I'm gonna go in the house and leave a note. Want some hot cocoa?" When Packrat didn't answer, I jiggled his sleeping bag until I heard a groan.

The lump started wiggling its way to the top of the bag. When his head emerged, Packrat opened one eye. His wavy hair was all staticky, and he had a bright red sleep mark down one side of his face.

"I'm going in for cocoa," I said.

Packrat mumbled before ducking back into the bag.

I hoped he wouldn't fall asleep again.

Inside, I could smell Mom's coffee brewing and heard the shower running. Putting on a kettle to boil water, I found the most effective Wilder family communication tool in the whole house: a pad of paper on the kitchen counter. Not only was it looked at by everybody coming and going through the kitchen door, but it was also proof that we'd told somebody something, in the event that they forgot we'd told them.

It'd saved me from being grounded for life a few times.

I ripped off two three-day-old messages that Mom and Dad had written back and forth about who was cooking supper, and when, and then ripped off yesterday's note from Dad to me, about where to meet him to do the trash run. On a clean sheet of paper, I wrote:

Sunday morning. Gone kayaking with Packrat to see loons. Back by 8 to do a bathroom check. I have my radio, but it's on low.

Coop

I dumped two packages of cocoa in each travel mug and filled them with hot water. I snapped the covers on, picked them up, took a sip from mine, and turned around. Hot cocoa almost came spewing out my nose when I saw Molly sitting at the counter, chin in her hands. When had she come in?

"Where ya going?" she asked.

"Out in the kayaks with Packrat. Tell Mom we'll be back by the time she opens the store."

"Can I come?"

I frowned at her. "Mom and Dad would kill me if I took you out."

"I can put my face in the water now. I'm ready to learn to swim. I am! But Mommy always says, 'Ask Daddy.' Daddy always says, 'Tomorrow.' " Molly dropped her arms and put her face in them.

Sighing, I looked out the kitchen window. Not seeing Packrat, I put down the cocoa mugs and asked Molly, "Want me to get you some cereal before I go?"

"I'm sick of cereal. I want Mom's special waffles."

"You know Mom can't make them. She doesn't have time." Molly looked up with her best do-it-for-your-favorite-little-sister look. "I can't. Packrat's waiting for me," I said.

39

Head in her arms again, she mumbled, "Nobody ever has time for me anymore. Not even you."

I sighed, got her favorite pink bowl from the dishwasher, and shook a box of cereal next to her ear. "Looo-oook. I have Crispy Chocolate Flakes."

Molly lifted her head just enough to peek over her arms. Sugar cereals were usually banned from our house, but when the campground got busy and Mom cooked less, those sugar cereals somehow magically appeared in the cupboard. I called it "guilt cereal." But not to Mom's face. I didn't want that chocolate cereal replaced with plain oatmeal.

Once I saw Molly was settled, happily watching cartoons, swinging her legs, and chowing down Crispy Chocolate Flakes, I took Packrat his cocoa. A few more nudges and putting the cocoa under his nose got him up and out of the tent, putting on his coat, and slowly stumbling toward the lake.

Woou-ou-ou-ou.

The loons' tremolo call had Packrat's eyes wide open and his feet moving into a slow jog. In the early-morning quiet, I thought our footsteps on the hard-packed dirt road sounded more like a herd of wild horses.

"Whatever was bugging them last night is still bugging them this morning," I said to Packrat.

"Could be something new." Packrat shot me a glance.

Beakman's *I need to take care of something* popped into my head. I picked up the pace.

Only one or two campers from the tenting section were up, poking the embers from last night's campfire to get it going again. At the loons' calls they froze in place for a minute, smiled toward the lake, and then went back to moving embers around. My mouth watered, thinking about the bacon and eggs they'd probably be making for breakfast.

Reaching the beach, I unlocked the boathouse and grabbed two kayak paddles, two life jackets, and two keys. I tossed Packrat the key to the yellow kayak so he could unlock its chain from the tree. Then I unlocked my favorite, the dark green one.

Woou-ou-ou-ou.

We dragged our kayaks over to the boat launch at the end of the beach. A light fog hovered over the water, slowly drifting off to the left in the direction the water flowed.

Ahead of us, a big yellow glow-ball was trying to fight its way through the trees and the fog. Off to our right, gray clouds loomed in the distance. I wondered which one would rise over us first—the morning sun, or another rainstorm?

The snaps of our life jackets were all we heard for a minute or two as we rushed to get them on. When I finally looked up, I tried not to laugh. Packrat had put his trench coat on over the life jacket. We took off our sneakers, threw them in the kayaks, and rolled up our pants. I put my binoculars in the waterproof hatch behind the seat. Floating the boats in knee-deep water, we climbed in and shoved off.

We'd only dipped our paddles in the water a few times when Packrat whispered, "Look! Look!"

The eagle was coming in fast, soaring downward, talons first. Opening them at the last second, it snatched a wiggling brown trout from the surface before rising back into the air, heading for its nest.

"That," Packrat said, "was worth getting up for."

I grinned at him. Seeing stuff like that almost every day was definitely the coolest thing about living here.

"Head over there," I said, pointing toward the long skinny island in front of us. "Ant Island."

Packrat laughed. "Is that its real name?"

"The camp kids call it that 'cause it's covered from one end to the other with anthills." I gave him a sideways grin. "Don't ever take a picnic lunch there!"

We paddled in time with each other, dipping one side of the paddle, then the other, into the water. Eventually, the low hum of a motorboat broke the stillness. A little speck on the right was moving toward us fast.

"Roy." I groaned. "His stupid motor's always got to be wide open."

As Roy pulled closer, Packrat and I paddled nearer each other. Circling around us twice before killing the motor, Roy asked, "What are you two doing out here?"

"Homework. What's it look like?" I said, just wanting to get on with our loon search. My kayak was tipping crazily from side to side in the wake of Roy's boat, and I kept dipping my paddle in the water to try to keep the boat steady.

Roy's chin went up a notch. After a minute's stare-down, he bent over. Next thing I knew, he'd lifted his emergency oar up over his head. I didn't even have time to duck before he'd dragged it across the surface of the lake to give me a face full of cold water.

Roy laughed, right before he did it again.

I took my paddle and threw water back. Roy sat higher up in his boat, so it was harder to get him back. Packrat paddled around me to join in the battle.

I admit, it might have been fun if it hadn't been Roy.

All the splashing and hollering and moving around in the boats brought us closer. Before I realized it, Roy's oar connected with my paddle and it was knocked from my hands.

For a second, nobody moved. I looked at Roy, then glanced at my kayak paddle floating in the water.

Roy looked at my paddle, then at me.

I looked at Roy again.

Roy looked at the paddle.

I moved first.

Paddling the water with both hands, I tried to pull my kayak closer to my paddle.

Roy was quicker. With his oar, he dragged my paddle to his boat and pulled it inside to raise over his head like a hard-won trophy.

"Give it back!" I wanted to lunge from the kayak and rip that paddle out of his hands the way the eagle had pulled the trout from the lake. But lunging and kayaks don't go so well together. I'd found that out once when I had stretched for a soda can floating in the water and ended up rolling over.

Nope. No lunging. That left only one option.

I let out a huge sigh. "What's the bet, Roy?"

"I bet that even if I give you a five-minute head start, you won't reach the dock before I get there. If you get there first, you get your paddle back."

"And if you get there first?" I asked, afraid of the answer.

"You have to walk around the pool like a chicken for fifteen minutes on the Saturday of Memorial Day weekend. When it's busiest."

"You've got to be kidding." I looked behind me at Packrat. He shrugged.

Roy quickly said, "And you can't use Packrat's kayak paddle."

I shot back, "You can't use your motor."

Roy laughed. "Got me. But I can still beat you."

"You promise I get a five-minute head start?"

Roy nodded toward Packrat. "You can make him timekeeper if you want. I'm sure he's got a waterproof clock in that stupid coat."

"Deal," I said, reluctantly.

Roy smiled. "Deal."

Suddenly, Roy's gaze moved quickly from me to Packrat. He frowned.

Packrat had a hand down inside the collar of his jacket. He straightened his upper body, twisted it slightly to the left, and pulled out a two-foot-long canoe paddle. "You didn't say I couldn't give him this."

Roy laughed. "So what? It'll take hours for him to get back to shore with that dinky thing."

Packrat put a hand on either end of the paddle and unfolded it to make it four feet. No one said a word as we all heard it click into place.

"Your new friend," said Roy, jabbing a finger toward Packrat, "is a freak!"

Packrat waggled the paddle. "A freak with a paddle."

Roy growled, "Deal's off." He threw my kayak paddle into the water before pulling the cord to his motor. His mouth moved a mile a minute. I couldn't hear a word he was saying, but it didn't take a lip reader to know. Finally, he put it in gear and motored away.

I shook my head as Packrat glided over, scooping up my paddle on the way. I raised an eyebrow. "What took you so long?"

Packrat shrugged. "I wanted to see what kind of weird bet he'd come up with this time."

Chapter 9

Loons' legs are at the back of their bodies. This makes them clumsy on land, but it's also what makes them very strong swimmers.

Packrat and I were really soaked from the water battle with Roy. Our T-shirts were sticking to our skin and I had goose bumps on my goose bumps. But I knew that if I went back home to change, Mom would catch me and tell me I didn't have time to go back on the lake. So we kept heading for Ant Island.

As we rounded its left point, I paddled closer to Packrat and said, "Let's drift here. If one of the parents is still on the nest and we scare it off, it might kick its own eggs into the water by accident."

We laid our paddles across the kayak openings in front of us. I took my binoculars from the kayak hatch, while Packrat slid his from a coat pocket.

"What am I looking for?" he asked.

"The nest is right on the edge of the shore, and it blends in pretty good. It'll be about a three-foot-wide mound with brownish grasses, and maybe small leaves and twigs. The loon might be lying with its neck on the ground to hide from us. . . . What the—?" I blurted, taking the binoculars away from my eyes. Blinking a few times, I raised them again.

Both loons were in the water, which was weird. There's always one on the eggs, keeping them warm. Instead, they were poking at the nest, moving old reeds and twigs with their beaks.

"It's almost like . . . like they're trying to push the nest back, out of the water," I said. Focusing my old, cracked binoculars on the two

unprotected olive-colored eggs the best I could, I saw the reason why
they were working so hard. "The water's up in the nest!"

"Can't they just push the eggs back farther, or carry them or
something?"

"No. They're clumsy on land." Lowering my binoculars, I looked
back toward the end of the lake. "Maybe something's blocking the outlet
on the old dam. I know it's been raining a lot, but still . . ."

The early morning fog had lifted, and we could see all around the
lake now, but the promise of a sunny day had gone too. The clouds had
won the race above us, hiding the sun. Light rain began to fall.

As we paddled to the dam, I showed Packrat how most of the land around the lake was ours. The only section that wasn't was the north end. The dam was there, with three houses to the right of it, and an undeveloped chunk owned by someone we'd never met on the left.

When the old dam came into view, I couldn't believe my eyes. A two-foot-wide board had been jammed into the dip of the dam, where the water usually funneled out of Pine Lake into a small stream.

"Aww, c'mon!" I slammed a fist on the side of the kayak. "There hasn't been a board in the top of the dam since we moved here. The neighbors let the first one rot away because they liked the water down low. Who'd put a new one in now?"

Packrat and I paddled the kayaks through a bunch of floating logs to get over to the dam. We dragged our kayaks up onto land, took off our coats and life jackets, and dropped them inside the boats. I led the way as we gingerly stepped over some rocks, then walked single file along a short, wide, crumbling cement wall. The water gently flowed over the top of the board and fell into the little creek below. This was way different from its usual waterfall rush.

I rolled up my shirtsleeves. "I'm pulling it out."

Packrat looked around. "Is that okay? I mean, what if the person who put it there is still around?"

"I don't care! The loons are losing their eggs."

We plunged our arms into the cold water to grab the bottom of the swollen board. We even worked at it with the hammer and screwdriver Packrat had pulled out of his pocket, until our elbows almost wouldn't bend, they were so stiff from the cold.

"It isn't going anywhere," I said, sitting back on my heels and wiping my wet bangs off my forehead.

Woou-ou-ou-ou.

Packrat and I stopped to listen, as the loons' tremolos became louder and faster.

"That doesn't sound good," Packrat said.

We climbed in our kayaks and headed back toward the call. It wasn't a pretty sight. The two loons were swimming this way and that in front of the nest. They seemed pretty upset. The water had half-covered one egg and was sneaking up on the second. And as if that wasn't bad enough, the clouds opened up and a heavier rain started to fall.

I muttered, "Could this morning get any worse?"

Immediately, my radio crackled. "Cooper?" Mom said. "Are you heading back?"

I looked at Packrat and sighed.

Mom kept talking. "It's eight o'clock. Dad had to fix the water hookup on a site. Someone accidentally chopped it with their wood ax in the dark last night, and it's turned the site next to it into a pond. So you have to do a bathroom check by yourself, I'm afraid."

Suddenly, I was glad she'd called. "Mom, can you call Warden Kate?" I quickly explained about the board and the loons.

"I don't think the warden—"

"Trust me! She'll want to know. There's an extra board in the dam. The water's rising fast." When she finally agreed, I told her we'd be right in. I wanted to know what Warden Kate would have to say about this.

The loons were diving, popping back up twenty yards away, wailing mournfully, then diving again.

"I can't just sit here and watch!" Packrat said. "Let's just pick up the eggs and move them!"

"Don't you think I would if I could?" I shot back. "If we touch them, they'll reject them." More gently I added, "Besides, without the loons sitting on them and the cold water around them, they're probably already . . . you know . . ."

Packrat's shoulders slumped and he faced the loons again. My eyes stung as I watched the loons losing their battle to save their family.

"Sorry," I mumbled.

"For what?" Packrat asked, not turning around.

"For yelling at you. For showing you this. It's a downer, I know."

Packrat slowly turned to look at me, a puzzled look on his face. "It's a downer, yeah. But kind of cool to see nature in action at the same time, you know?"

I did know. "So you aren't sorry you came?"

"Nah." Packrat wiped his cheek with his sleeve, to get rid of rain or a tear, I wasn't sure which. "But this has to be the saddest thing I've ever seen."

Chapter 10

Adult loons mostly like to be alone or with their mate, but will sometimes get together in groups of twenty to thirty, to hang out. Called "rafting," this usually happens in early morning or late afternoon, from midsummer to September.

That same night, Packrat and I sat by the campfire. Mom and Dad had a circle of benches and chairs in a small clearing behind the office. Mom said it was kind of like the campground living room. They'd light a roaring, crackling fire in the big metal ring that sat in the middle of the circle. Weekenders, weeklies, seasonals . . . It didn't matter how long you'd been camping at Wilder Family Campground, or even how long you were staying; everyone was invited. Sometimes only Mom and Dad sat there, talking about their day. Other times, like this Sunday night, the circle was full.

"They're calling for sun tomorrow," Dad said, nudging the logs in the fire with his poking stick. "Temps in the low seventies. Not a minute too soon, either. I swear I'm growing moss between my toes from working in this damp weather."

I groaned quietly. Dad's told that joke at every campfire since we opened on May 1. I can't believe anybody still laughs when he tells it. But they do.

Someone answered, "Of course the sun'll come out tomorrow. I have to go back to the office."

A third camper laughed. "You could always call in sick," he said.

Dad and I shared a smile over the campfire. We never had to worry about getting stuck indoors on a beautiful day.

I figured it was time for me to go in the house since I had school tomorrow, and last-minute homework to do, when *plop!* A bag of marshmallows dropped on my sneakers.

There was Packrat, elbow deep in a pocket again. On the bench between us was a package of graham crackers and four bars of chocolate.

"What are you looking for?" I asked.

"The sticks," he said. "Reusable ones. You know, to save a tree and all that?"

I laughed.

He pulled out two telescoping metal roasting sticks, handed one to me, then waved his in the air and called out, "Who wants me to make them an end-of-the-weekend s'more?"

He was everyone's hero.

Dad threw another log on the fire. When it stuck outside the rim a little too far, he kicked it deeper into the flames with the toe of his boot. Bright orange sparks floated up toward the early-evening sky. Big Joe from the Snack Shack liked to say those sparks were stars going up to take their place in heaven.

Holding the plastic handle, I slid a marshmallow on the forked end of the roasting stick before lowering it into the fire, as close to the coals as I could get it without touching them. When it burst into flames right away like I wanted it to, I blew it out. I touched the marshmallow once, twice, before deciding it was cool enough to pull off the blackened skin and pop it in my mouth. Then I put the rest of the marshmallow back into the fire to do it all over again.

I was on my third when Mom came walking into the circle. She handed Dad a coffee mug, then sat beside him to sip from her own.

"Cooper? Did you tell your father what you saw this morning—about the loons losing their eggs?"

"Yep," I said, keeping my eyes on my marshmallow. He'd squeezed my shoulder and given me the it's-nature-in-action-so-what-can-we-do talk. What I didn't tell them was that I thought it was all their fault. If they'd just let me go out on my patrol days ago, I might have seen the board before the water level had risen, and been able to tell the game warden about it. Or if Dad had come with me, maybe he could have pulled it out.

Mr. Beakman leaned forward. His nose reflected the orange glow of the fire. "I say, good! Who needs more loons out on the lake? They're a big nuisance, anyhow." He sat back in his chair. Both sides of his lips slowly lifted upward. "Yeah. Maybe they'll move on. Fish somewhere else. Stop bothering people."

"The loons can't leave," I said. "People camp here so they can hear them wailing at night. They want to watch them dive and nest and stuff. If the loons leave, our campers might leave, too."

There was a lot of feet shuffling and coughing. Mom and Dad shared a look over the campfire. Everyone looked everywhere but at Mr. Beakman, or me.

"I think," Mr. Beakman said slowly, "that it's kind of out of your hands."

Before I could say anything, voices rang out from all sides of the campfire.

"Uh-oh!"

"It's going to fall!"

"Careful!"

"Watch it!"

While we'd been talking, Packrat had been slowly twirling a marshmallow over and over, high above the shimmering red coals. It was lightly browned, and drooping way low by one thin marshmallow

thread. Another round of gasps rang out, until he finally pulled it from the fire.

Packrat slid the marshmallow off the stick onto a graham cracker topped with a piece of chocolate bar. Putting another graham cracker on top, he squished them together until the marshmallow oozed out on all four sides. He sighed and said "Mmm-mmm-mmm," before shoving half of it in his mouth.

He did this twice, before I couldn't stand it anymore and tried it his way. He just made it look so good.

"Hey, Packrat," I said with a mouthful of s'more. "You know you can make these with peppermint patties? Or white chocolate? Or peanut-butter cups?"

Packrat stopped, a s'more halfway to his mouth. "Peanut-butter cups?" His eyes widened. "Whoa. My favorite. We'll have to try that next time."

"Aha!" I said, waving what was left of my marshmallow sandwich in his face. "You don't have a peanut-butter cup in one of your pockets, do you?"

He frowned. "Huh?"

"You said you'd make a peanut-butter s'more *next time*. If you had a peanut-butter cup *now*, you'd make one tonight!"

My grin drooped like one of Packrat's overcooked marshmallows when he dug a peanut-butter cup out of his pocket. "Nah—I have one. But I'm out of graham crackers."

I almost had him that time. I was about to tell him so, too, when I heard a squeaky-voiced lady across from me mention something about loons and nests and second chances.

Second chances? For the loons? I leaned forward.

"I'm telling you, Sam, I read it somewhere . . . where was it? *Wild-life Weekly?* No, no, that can't be it, because we haven't gotten that magazine for some time."

I wanted to jump up and say, "Who cares where you saw it, lady? What did the article say?" But she was still talking, not even taking a breath between sentences, so there was no way to do the customer-service thing without interrupting.

I bit my tongue. Hard.

She must have just checked in today or something, 'cause I didn't recognize her, or her voice. She was really, really thin, with long gray hair in a ponytail. She wore a long necklace made with big blue beads that clicked together when she moved her head from side to side.

"*Nature's Way?*" she guessed again. "Hmmm . . . that could be it. How long have we been getting that magazine, Sam? Three months? Four?"

She paused. I leaned forward to ask my question, but a man's voice beat me to it. "Marcia. Please. Just tell us what the article said."

The woman harrumphed. "I only thought they might want to know, Sam. In case they want to look it up or something."

Listen to Sam—please! I begged in my mind.

"The article said loons will try to lay a second set of eggs if the first set doesn't hatch."

Mr. Beakman barked, "A second set?"

"Well. Yes." Squeaky Lady's eyes darted from Sam, who I guessed was her husband, to my father, to Mr. Beakman, fearfully, and back to her husband again. When he nodded encouragingly, she went on. "You know how the first set of eggs usually hatches around the end of May, or Memorial Day weekend?" When everyone nodded, she continued. "Well, if that nest fails, sometimes they'll try again. Those babies will be born around Fourth of July week. This makes it dangerous for the babies because lots of boaters are out during the holiday, and—"

Mr. Beakman cut her off with a wave of his hand. "Babies, schmabies! I'm telling you, we don't need another set of loons, wailing their sad song and luring people to the lake."

"Hey there, campers! Can I join you for a bit?" said a voice from the darkness outside the circle.

Everyone breathed a sigh of relief so heavy, I swear the campfire flickered. Dad quickly said, "Everyone, this is our friend Tom. He lives on the north side of the lake, and he's our resident celebrity."

Squeaky Lady exclaimed, "Oh! Tom! I've seen you on that *Community Connections* show."

"That's the one." Tom tipped his baseball cap with the moose on it at her. "Thanks for watching."

Dad pointed toward an empty chair. "Have a seat, Tom. Did you boat over tonight?"

Tom nodded, and got comfortable in his chair. With a new person joining the group, the conversation returned to the weather and Dad's toes.

I was about to kick Packrat's foot so we could go find something better to do, when Tom said, "I know this rain must be bad for business, Jim, but I kind of like the way the lake's filling up. Maybe that'll keep me from losing another motor to the weeds, like I did last year."

Maybe all Mr. Beakman's loon-bashing had put me on the edge of freaking out, and Tom's comment just pushed me over. I don't know. Before I knew it, I was blurting in a very un-customer-service-like way, "But it stinks for the animals that live on the lake! It stinks for the loons!"

When no one said a word, I got embarrassed and looked at the tip of my sneaker, which was now digging a hole in the dirt.

Tom squinted my way. "Cooper! Didn't see you there! How's my favorite game warden in training?"

I was glad Tom wasn't mad at me. He tipped his head to one side and frowned. "What did you say about the loons?"

"Their nest flooded this morning," I said. "Someone put a board in the dam."

Big Joe asked me, "Hey, why don't I just take you over there and help take it out?"

"Warden Kate said I can't. It's too late for the loon eggs now. And she's worried other animals might have nested since the water went up. If we drop the water level too fast, it might confuse them." Looking out the side of my eyes toward Mr. Beakman, I added, "She's investigating to find out who did it."

Mr. Beakman shifted in his seat. Dad raised an eyebrow.

Tom leaned forward, putting his elbows on his knees. "Cooper, you're sure it's from the board in the old dam? Not all the rain?"

I shrugged my shoulders. "Well, the warden said it's kind of both."

Tom stared at the campfire. He sighed deeply. "That's a shame. I can't remember when the loons haven't had a baby born—"

Woo-OOOOO-ooo. Woo-OOOOO-ooo.

Everyone's heads tipped slightly toward the sound, listening to the loon parents wailing their sorrow to all who would listen.

"Such a sad call," my mother said. "It's hard to lose someone you love."

Mr. Beakman looked quickly at my mother. "Loons know nothing of love, or losing, Joan." He patted his chest. "Humans feel deeply. Animals go on instinct."

Woo-OOOOO-ooo.

My mother shrugged. "Explain that call, then."

Dad said, "Tom, you've been on this lake longer than the rest of us. Have you ever known the loons to nest a second time?"

"Well," Squeaky Lady said in a hushed voice, "remember, they have to lose both eggs before the instinct to re-nest kicks in. If they've always had babies, like Tom said . . ."

This time I did kick Packrat's shoe, and got up to leave. Before we'd gotten outside the glow of the flames, Mom called me back. Whispering so she wouldn't disturb the other conversations, she said, "I've got to go back to the store and do some paperwork. Be in the house by eight. Check on Molly for me. Bed by nine."

"But Mom, it's already seven-thirty!" I picked up the baby monitor sitting on Mom's armrest and put it to my ear. "And Molly's snoring! She's fine. Can I at least wait with Packrat until he goes home?"

Mom looked toward Molly's bedroom window across the road and sighed. "You've got ten minutes, tops. It's a school night, and school comes first. Packrat will be back next weekend. Besides," Mom said, narrowing her eyes playfully, "my mom-radar tells me there's some homework that needs doing."

Packrat and I turned toward the game room. I wasn't surprised to see it empty. Spring and fall, it only got used on weekend nights. Once school let out, though, and families stayed for whole weeks, kids would be hanging out the windows and off the porch railing every night.

"How much longer do you have?" I asked.

"A couple minutes. I told Mom to pick me up here when she was done checking on Grandma and had the camper closed up. These quarters are burning a hole in my pocket." Pulling one of his pockets inside out, he slipped his pinky through a tiny tear in the bottom, chuckling at his own joke.

As Packrat banged on the flippers of an old pinball machine and set the ball whizzing around the hoops and tracks, I leaned on the machine and wondered aloud, "Did you notice Mr. Beakman was real quiet after I said Warden Kate was investigating?"

"Kind of." Packrat kept his eye on the ball as the points added up on the screen. *Ding. Ding. Ding, ding, ding.*

"I bet he's the one who put the board in the dam," I said. "He raised the water level of the lake and drowned the loon eggs. That was the other something he had to do."

"He makes a good suspect." *Ding, ding. Ding, ding, ding.* "But you said Roy's on the lake a lot." *Ding, ding.* "He was on the lake that day, too." *Ding, ding, ding.*

"Yeah," I said.

We watched silently as Packrat's ball slipped right between the two outstretched flippers.

Chapter 11

Common loons weigh about nine pounds and have a three-foot wingspan. The males are 20 percent larger than the females.

Man, the next week was long. Through my classes at school and my campground chores, all I could think about were those loons. Game Warden Kate e-mailed to say she'd collected the water-covered eggs so the loons wouldn't hang out around them. They'd lost their family, thanks to some jerk putting that board in the dam.

I'd give anything for them to re-nest, like Squeaky Lady had said. But if they did, and then the same jerk took the board out, would they have trouble getting to their nest and lose a second family?

It was only the third weekend of May, but I was stinky sweaty doing the Saturday-morning trash run. So when Packrat's mom's car finally drove in and he called out the window, "Do you want to go swimming?," I said, "Sure! I just have to tell Mom."

Mom wasn't so sure. "Don't be silly. The water isn't warm enough for that." She was playing around with a window fan so that it would blow on her behind the counter.

"C'mon. It's ninety degrees out!" I knew from having looked at myself in the bathroom mirror that my face was beet-red. Hoping it might help, I made her look at me by getting in her way every time she turned around.

The camp phone rang. Mom waved me aside so she could get to the phone and the computer station. "Wilder Family Campground. Joan speaking. Can I help you?"

I draped myself over the counter next to her and sighed. Mom babbled on about how many people could fit on a site, and asked them what they were camping in. I gave her my I'm-so-hot-and-stinky-sweaty-I'm-going-to-die-right-this-second look. She asked the person on the phone for a name and address while glaring at me. I put a hand to my throat, making a bunch of deep-throated hacking and choking sounds. She gave me her best knock-it-off look. I mouthed the words *waaaa-ter, waaaa-ter, waaaa-ter,* as I slowly, slowly, slowly sank to the floor.

Mom sweetly said into the mouthpiece, as her eyes shot daggers at me, "Yes, yes. You can hear the loons at night. Excuse me, could you hold for one second, please?" She put a hand over the receiver and whispered, "You. Are. Driving. Me. Crazy! Go, already. But be back by two or—"

I never heard the end of that sentence.

Packrat and I raced to the shoreline with our floats. Reaching the beach first, I tossed my towel on a tree branch and threw my inner tube into the lake as far as I could. I ran into the water up to my waist and dived in headfirst. I popped up through the middle of my tire float, gasping for air.

Mom was right. The water was cold! Not that I'd tell her that.

I pulled myself through the middle of the ring until I was lying across the top of it, my butt in the water, my hands lazily paddling me in slow circles. The sun beating on the black of the tube had me warm again in minutes. The perfect spot on the perfect day.

When I looked back toward the beach, Packrat was in the water up to his knees. He had his camouflage-colored blowup boat in front of him. He carefully climbed in, his coat still on. When he'd hand-paddled out beside me, I asked, "Don't you ever take that off?"

"When it's warm enough." He lay back and shut his eyes. His coat flopped open to show just a blue bathing suit underneath.

As we soaked up the sun and floated around, we talked about school. We talked about friends. We talked about our teachers. Turns out, Packrat was worried about seventh grade.

"I hear Mr. Winhart is strict," he said.

"You mean keep-the-floor-clean-under-your-desk strict?"

"Nah. More like he won't let me wear my coat into class because it will be . . . disruptive."

One hand making circles in the water, I snorted. "Yeah. Like a coat's disruptive."

When Packrat didn't say anything, I opened one eye to look at him. His face toward the sun, eyes closed, he wore a big grin.

"What?" I said, turning on my side. "Come on! Tell me!"

He laughed. "I got my coat at the start of fourth grade. I wanted to be a detective for Halloween, you know? So Grandpa took me to our church's used-clothing store." Packrat tugged a collar. "It dragged on the floor, but I didn't care.

"I loaded every pocket with something, put on a detective hat, and carried a notebook. Kids played this game with me, guessing what I had in my pockets. It was voted best costume in my class *and* at the town party that night," he said proudly. "I liked the coat so much, I wore it the next day. And the next. And the next.

"Every morning I loaded it with the stuff I thought I'd need that day. Even my lunch. At night, some stuff stayed, some came out."

"Like a backpack," I said.

"And my teacher was pretty cool about it too. Until . . ." Packrat chuckled.

"Just tell it already!" I said.

"On Grandparents Day, we were supposed to share one thing from home with the class and our visiting grandparents. I wanted to share my pet rat, Bo, because my grandparents had given him to me. I put him in a pocket and buttoned it shut."

"He chewed his way through the pocket," I guessed.

"Not the pocket," Packrat hinted. "A couple weeks before, I'd packed a tuna sandwich in that same pocket for lunch. But the cafeteria was serving pizza, so I had that instead, and forgot about the sandwich."

I frowned, not quite getting what he was saying.

"The sandwich was still there, and Bo found it."

I threw my head back and laughed.

Packrat chuckled too. "When it was my turn to share, I unbuttoned the pocket to pull out Bo, and you should've seen it!" Packrat crossed his arms behind his head and looked toward the sky with a faraway gaze. "My teacher and some girls screamed and jumped on their chairs. The rest of the girls ran to the back of the room. Then they all stopped, sniffed the air, and blocked their noses. Man, my eyes were watering, that sandwich smelled so bad."

It took a while before I could stop laughing long enough to ask, "So, did they make you leave your coat at home after that?"

"Nah. Ms. Marco was really cool about it, once she'd calmed down." Packrat put a hand over his heart. "I had to swear to no animals, insects, or reptiles in the pockets. I had to empty my pockets of food every night. Grandpa took me home early that day because the smell was all over Bo and my clothes too. We rode home with the windows open."

Hoooot hoot.

Packrat and I quietly rolled onto our sides when we heard the loons' soft call. They silently glided along the shore's edge, softly hooting back and forth.

"You think they're looking for a new spot? Like Squeaky Lady said?" Packrat asked.

"Maybe," I said.

One of the loons put its face below the water's surface, looked back up, then quickly dived.

Neither one of us said a word while we waited for it to come back up. Finally, Packrat asked, "Where'd it go?"

"Loons can dive far," I said. "They stay underwater for close to two minutes. You never know where they'll come up. . . . There!" I said, pointing off to the right, about a hundred yards away. When the smaller of the two loons dove, I said, "Ha! She saw lunch."

"She?" Packrat asked. "How can you tell them apart?"

"It's hard. The male is just a little bit bigger, so I can only tell if I see them together."

The female loon popped back up. We watched the pair glide along together and then apart. Every time one of them dived, Packrat and I would take bets on where it'd come up next.

Packrat was winning by two quarters, when the roar of a motor interrupted our game. It was Roy again.

He killed the motor about three hundred yards from us. Looking our way, he nodded once, picked up his fishing pole from the bottom of his boat, and cast out in the other direction.

Packrat and I looked at each other with our eyebrows raised.

When it looked as if Roy was going to ignore us, Packrat and I flopped on our backs. Laying in the warm sun, listening to the soft hooting of the loons and feeling my float rock gently beneath me, I began to get sleepy. The breeze softly blew, and I heard the newly budded leaves rustling.

Woou-ou-ou-ou. Woou-ou-ou-ou.

I rolled over so fast, I almost fell off my float. The loon on the left was between land and Roy. The other one, behind him, had stretched out its neck across the water to give its crazy laugh. Suddenly, with wings flapping and water splashing, it raced across the water toward Roy.

Roy scooted as far away from that loon as he could get without leaving his boat.

The loon dived before reaching him. The loon to Roy's left took up the tremolo call where its mate had left off.

Roy scrambled back to the middle of the boat. His eyes had gotten huge and were darting between the pair.

I cupped my hands around my mouth. "Roy! Just paddle away!"

The loon to Roy's right had resurfaced away from him, only to stretch its neck out across the water and race at him again like a bull toward a red cape. Roy glanced my way.

I yelled, "It's okay! He's just telling you you're too close. Don't be scared."

The minute the words popped out of my mouth, I knew they were the wrong ones. Roy's eyes lost that nervous look and hardened instead. He put down his pole and picked up his emergency oar.

Then he raised the oar over his head.

"No!" Packrat and I yelled at the same time.

Roy slammed it down into the water, splashing the loon. It reared back on its feet and spread its wings to show a dazzling display of white. Bill on its chest, the loon frantically danced on top of the water.

Roy raised the oar again.

And brought it down again.

"You'll scare it to death! Its heart can't take it!" I yelled. "Back off!"

When Roy raised the oar a third time, I took a deep breath. Knowing I'd probably pay for this later, I yelled, "Roy! Mess with the loons again and I'll tell the game warden! I'm betting you won't want to pay that five-hundred-dollar fine!"

I heard a click. Packrat had pulled a waterproof camera out of his coat and taken Roy's picture.

Roy stopped in mid-swing. He stared at us.

Packrat whispered, "I shouldn't have done that, huh?"

I swallowed. Lots of times.

The loons had gotten together and quickly dived. I didn't look to see where they'd come up this time. I was too busy keeping my eyes on Roy.

He'd put the oar down and grabbed hold of the pull cord on his motor. He flexed his fingers a couple of times before yanking on it so hard, he almost fell overboard. His motor roared, then sputtered, and died. If he'd been in the water, I wouldn't have been surprised if it had boiled around him.

Roy yanked the pull cord again. All this time, he hadn't taken his eyes off us.

The motor roared to life. Roy grabbed hold of the rudder and turned the boat toward us.

When he was two hundred yards away, I glanced toward shore. No way could we get there on the floats before he reached us.

Packrat said quietly, "He wouldn't . . . would he?"

"Nah," I said. I wasn't quite sure I believed it, though.

When Roy was a hundred yards away, my heart started pounding out of my chest. I said to Packrat, "Get ready to bail."

Roy kept his eyes glued to mine. When he was fifty yards away, the roar of the motor sunk into my skull, making it hard to think. I could smell gas fumes as he bore down on us.

Packrat grabbed both sides of his float.

I opened my mouth to give the signal at the same time that Roy lifted his chin and steered sharply off to our right, spraying us in lake water.

I waited until I was sure he wasn't coming back before I fell back on my tube. "Whoa," was all I could think to say.

"Big wake!" Packrat warned. I grabbed hold of the sides of my inner tube so I wouldn't get tossed off by the waves. Packrat laughed. "Right up and over them. Too bad Ant Island doesn't float like this."

I froze. "Say that again?"

"Umm . . . big wake?"

I shook my head.

"Too bad Ant Island doesn't float—"

"Yes!" I sat up. "You're a brain! That's what we'll do!"

Packrat blinked several times. "We're going to make Ant Island float?"

"No, but we can make a raft that looks like a loon-size island. I saw it done on Animal Planet once. These volunteers got together to make three or four rafts because they said the really big motorboats kept swamping the loon nests. They put plants on the rafts and anchored them out in the lake and . . . we can do that!" I grinned. "It's perfect. The loons will stay to make a new family, the campers will come to listen to the loons, Mom and Dad will take my patrols seriously, and maybe they'll even want to come out in the canoe with me once a week!"

Packrat pulled a hammer and a screwdriver from his pockets. "Count me in! When do we start?"

Chapter 12

Loons stretch their wings a lot. When they do, if their bills point upward, they are probably not feeling threatened. When their bills are down, back away.

"Sure, I have all the supplies for this, Cooper." Dad held the sketch I'd drawn of the loon raft last night. Packrat and I had found this great website with directions and a couple of different ways to do it. I tried to find plans that I knew we had all the stuff for.

Dad tipped back his ball cap and tapped my plans with his pointer finger. "Warden Kate must have told you this kind of thing usually has to be out in the wild for weeks or months first, right? The smell of humans being on it and all. The loons probably won't use it this year."

"Yeah, but she said it was worth a try." I took a deep breath and gave it a shot. "Want to help me?"

"I can't, Cooper. This roof needs replacing."

Why was I not surprised?

"But Packrat and I can raid your workshop?" I gave him my aren't-I-your-favorite-son look.

Dad laughed. "Sure. Raid away. Have fun making your . . . raft. But first—"

I sighed. "I know, I know. Clean the bathrooms."

Dad started back up the ladder.

"You're not helping?" I asked, shading my eyes with one hand to look up at him.

"I've got to get this done before the next batch of rain rolls in." He looked down at me and winked. "You know how to clean them, Coop."

Sure, I knew how to do it. But lately there were only two times I got to hang out with Dad. One was when we were cleaning bathrooms. Two was when we did the trash run.

Shaking off the gloom, I tossed my sketchpad on the workshop steps. Then I ran full speed toward the bathrooms, stopping only to grab my secret weapon from Mom's garden pond. The sooner I got those bathrooms done, the sooner the raft would get built.

Our bathrooms were in a big rectangular building. The men's and ladies' room doors were on the short ends. In the middle of a long side was the door to the maintenance room. From there, I could get into both sets of bathrooms without going all the way around the building, lugging mops, brooms, cleaners, and buckets.

Stopping to unlock the maintenance-room door, I heard heavy breathing behind me.

"Need a hand?" Packrat asked.

My mouth dropped open so far a bat could have flown in. Would other kids stock soda for a free can? Sure. Stack wood because they'd be riding the only golf cart in the campground? You bet. But ask them to scrub filthy toilets, wipe the soap scum and hair out of sinks and showers? Mop muddy floors dotted with toilet-paper scraps that have been who knows where? Ha! I'd have better luck asking, "Hey! Want to come to my house for supper? Mom's cooking eggplant parmesan and then my parents are gonna play the accordion for us."

Yeah. It was *that* bad.

But here was Packrat, pulling rubber gloves from a pocket, ready to help do the grossest job in the camp.

"Thanks," I said. "I think you're crazy. But thanks!"

The maintenance room had gray cement-block walls. There were a dozen shelves that held toilet-paper rolls, paper towels, and cleaning products. One corner had a very deep sink for washing out mops, buckets, and sponges. On my left was a door to the men's room that could only be opened from inside the maintenance room. On the right was the door to the ladies' room.

I knocked on the ladies' room door. "I'm here to clean!" I yelled.

We heard a lot of groaning, a few giggles, and some grumbling. One rude lady shouted back, "I just got in here!"

I grabbed a mop and a rolling bucket and headed into the men's room.

"But? You—" Packrat looked back toward the ladies' room door. "You just told them you were gonna clean in there."

"Have you ever seen how much junk they bring with them? Blow-dryers, makeup, curling irons, hair straighteners, and stuff, I don't even know what it is. Geez. I gave a warning, and if we're lucky, they'll be outta there in half an hour. Guys' room first."

I set up Packrat to scrub and rinse the showers. I swished the toilets with the toilet brush, refilled the toilet-paper dispensers, and emptied the trash buckets. Packrat then wiped down the sinks and mirrors. I mopped the floor, starting at the outside door and working my way backwards toward the maintenance room.

Suddenly, the outside door swung open.

"We're closed for cleaning," I said, not bothering to look up.

"Looks like you're done to me."

Roy walked right over my clean floor and reached for a stall door.

"Hey!" I yelled. "I said we're closed. And I just mopped this floor."

Roy looked at the floor, then nodded. "Great job. You'll make some girl a nice wife someday."

That did it. I threw my mop to the ground and started toward him with my fists clenched. Packrat got between us. "C'mon, Coop. He's kidding." Standing in my way, he looked over his shoulder to Roy. "Right? You were kidding?"

"Yeah. Ha, ha, ha. Making a joke. Can I pee now?"

Roy didn't wait for an answer. He just went into the stall. I pushed Packrat away from me and picked up the mop. Shaking the handle at him, I whispered, "What'd you do that for?"

"You wanted to whale on him. He's twice your size. You figure it out." Packrat walked out into the maintenance room.

I stared after him for a minute. He was right, of course. Roy would have been mopping the floor with me if Packrat hadn't gotten in the way.

I put the mop in the rolling bucket and pulled it along behind me, shutting the door to the maintenance room behind me. Packrat was listening at the girls' room door. I went up behind him.

"Hey. Sorry. That guy just knows how to make me see red."

"More like he's made that his life's mission, to *always* make you see red," he said. "He's messing with your head."

Yeah. That's exactly what it was like. Is like.

Packrat raised his eyebrows as he pointed at the gray steel door. "I still hear blow dryers."

I put my key in the lock and jiggled it around as a kind of a warning. "Bathroom cleaners are here!"

Squeals and rushing around could be heard. Then a familiar squeaky voice said, "You stop right there, young man. I'll be five more minutes. Ten, tops."

Packrat groaned.

"Watch and learn," I said, grabbing my bullfrog, Oscar, from the deep sink where I'd stashed him earlier.

"He's only got three legs!" Packrat exclaimed as he reached out to run a finger down Oscar's back.

"I rescued him after he was run over by a bike, and put him in Mom's garden. He can't go far, but he eats good." Rubbing my finger between Oscar's eyes, I said, "Do your stuff, boy."

I put Oscar on the floor in front of the door and quietly turned the door handle until it opened a crack. I gently nudged him from behind until he slid himself into the bathroom, and then I shut the door.

I held up five fingers, and bent them one by one. "Five, four, three, two, one—"

"Frog!" yelled a lady.

"Wh-wh-where?" screeched another. Blow dryers were turning off and now you could hear what sounded like towels and makeup being tossed in bags.

"Oh, for heaven's sake, it's just a bullfrog," said Squeaky Lady. "It won't hurt you."

It was quiet for a minute, then one by one, the blow dryers came on again and everyone started chatting and giggling.

Packrat said, "Well, that bombed. Now what?"

I didn't know. Whenever Oscar had accidentally-on-purpose gotten into the bathroom before, girls had packed up their stuff and left within seconds. The only thing that cleared out the bathroom faster was—

I winked at Packrat.

Putting my head near the door, I shouted, "She's right. I'm sure that old bullfrog just wandered in to eat the spiders."

The screaming began again, with Squeaky Lady being the loudest of all.

It worked every time.

Chapter 13

About 85 percent of loon nests are built on some kind of island, either natural or man-made. This helps to prevent some land-based predators like raccoons and skunks from finding and harming the eggs.

Forty-five minutes later we were loading up the golf cart in front of Dad's workshop. Packrat stood in the doorway with my sketch, reading off the things we needed for the loon raft.

"It just says nails; no size?"

I stared at row upon row of jars filled with nails. One-quarter-inch nails with no head. Ten-inch nails with a head. And everything in between.

"Take the biggest ones," Packrat said. "And maybe some a couple of sizes smaller. We need a hammer, staple gun, and hand saw."

I started digging through all the junk thrown on Dad's workbench, and I do mean junk. As a matter of fact, the whole workshop was loaded with junk. He never threw anything out. "The minute I do," he'd say, "I'll need it." What he kept forgetting was that it didn't matter if he saved it, 'cause when he did need it, he'd never find it in this mess.

His mess was my treasure chest, though.

Arms loaded with nails and tools, I went out to put it all in the golf cart.

"What's next?"

Packrat had followed me outside. "Two anchors and twenty feet of rope for each one."

Finding enough rope was easy. Dad had coils of it hanging on the walls. I grabbed two. It took a little longer to find something to serve as anchors. Luckily, a past camper had left behind some half-blocks of cement, and Dad had thrown them behind the workshop. Perfect.

I dropped two of them into the back of the golf cart and rubbed my hands together to get the dirt off them. Hearing something, I looked up to find Mom standing there, arms crossed, tapping a foot.

"Hi?" I half asked, half said.

"Bullfrogs and spiders in the ladies' room. You know anything about that?"

I flinched. "Maaaaay-be." When Mom frowned, I blurted out, "All I did was tell them not to be afraid of Oscar and they freaked out."

Mom tipped her head to one side. "Oscar? Your bullfrog?" She put her hands on her hips. "How did he get in there?"

"I don't know."

"Really? Give me your best guess on why he'd leave my safe, bug-infested garden and crawl all the way down to the bathrooms? To the ladies' room, no less?"

I shrugged. "Toilet water and spiders?"

Packrat giggled, then coughed to cover it up.

Mom put up a hand and tried to hide a little smile. "Cooper Wilder. I know exactly what you've been doing to clear that ladies' room, but it wasn't a problem until today. We're too busy now. I had six angry women in my store, upset over what they called our 'spider problem.' "

I laughed. "Spider problem? I don't think so. Well, maybe there's a daddy longlegs or two. But they won't hurt you."

"Regardless, Cooper. You can't scare them with spiders anymore to get your way. Agreed?"

She didn't say anything about not using Oscar ever again. "Agreed," I said. "Now can I go? We've got a loon raft to build!"

Molly stood next to the golf cart on her tiptoes, trying to make herself tall enough to see in the back of it. "What's a loon raft?"

"Packrat and I are making a little island for the loons to build a nest on."

Molly stepped onto the golf cart and plopped herself on the front seat.

"Oh, no, you don't," I said, shaking my head.

"Cooper?" I could tell Mom was choosing her words carefully. "Molly's been with me in the store all morning. Couldn't she just tag along while you and Packrat do your game warden thing? So she could, you know, see something different for a change?"

I gave Packrat a see-what-I-mean-about-not-being-taken-seriously look, before answering Mom. "I can't. We have to canoe out for the logs that were floating by the dam." I knew she'd never allow Molly to go out on the lake with us.

Mom's eyes seemed sad, but her voice was happy for Molly's sake as she held out her hand and said, "Come on, little girl. You can help me in the store. We'll stock the toy section."

"But I want to save the loons." Molly's face got all scrunched up, and her mouth quivered as she looked up at me. "Just like . . . like . . . you."

Man, I hated it when she did that.

But at least *she* didn't think I was playing.

I got down on one knee. "Okay. There is this one thing you can help us with. But it isn't until the very end."

"Really?" Her blue eyes got bluer with excitement. "What is it?"

"We have to put some dirt on it, and plant real lake plants. Almost like a little garden."

Molly clasped her hands together. "Promise you'll call me?"

"Promise," I said. "But it won't be till after lunch."

She nodded and wiped her tears with the backs of her hands, making black streaks across the tops of her chubby cheeks. Giving me a hug around the neck, she skipped back to Mom.

"What's next?" I asked, a little embarrassed Packrat had seen that.

But Packrat didn't seem to notice, or he didn't care. He tapped his pencil on the paper and rechecked his list. "Nails, hammer, saw, staple gun, anchors, logs for the frame. Got it all now. We're good to go!" He stood on the golf cart.

I hesitated. "We're forgetting something."

"Like what?"

I snapped my fingers. "The floor. To put the dirt on."

"Plywood?"

"No." I walked around the outside of Dad's workshop till I found the roll of wire mesh I was looking for. I had to pull it up out of the leaves and dirt that had settled inside it, but it was good enough for the raft. "This is what's left from when Dad fenced the garden to keep the deer out." I threw it in the back of the golf cart, hopped in the driver's seat, and put the cart in reverse.

"But how will we keep the dirt from falling through the mesh holes?" Packrat wondered.

"You'll see," I said.

After towing back five logs that were floating by the dam, four for the sides and one to go across the middle, we dragged them up onto the beach as far away from the dock as we could. We cut the logs six feet long. We tried nailing the ends together, but even with the big nails we had, I just couldn't figure it out. Either the nails bent, or they weren't long enough to go through a whole log and into the other. I tried to call Dad, but he was still working on the roof.

While we were struggling, Big Joe came in from fishing, and he taught us how to notch the ends so they'd fit one inside the other like Lincoln Logs. It was so much easier to nail them that way.

We pulled the wire mesh over the bottom, careful to tuck under any sharp points that might hurt the loons when they crawled on or off.

Packrat and I were standing back, feeling pretty proud of ourselves, when I heard a crackling noise coming from his pocket.

Pulling out his radio, he said into it, "Hey, Mom. What's up?"

"Coming back for lunch? There's grilled cheese in the pan."

My stomach growled. Packrat smiled. "Can I bring Cooper?"

"Sure, I'll throw a couple more on. And let Cooper know his mom's looking for him. Something about a bathroom being out of toilet paper?"

I sighed. "Now my mom's finding me through your mom."

Packrat pushed the button on the radio. "We'll be right up."

He put the radio back in his pocket and pointed at the raft. "Think we can get it on the back of the golf cart?"

"What for?" I said, looking down the beach and seeing just one family making a sandcastle. "I'm starving. Let's just drag it into the bushes so it blends in. No one will bother it."

Chapter 14

Loons usually dive to about 30 feet deep, but they have been known to go as deep as 150 feet for their prey.

When we returned, the raft had been dragged halfway out of the bushes. Someone had pulled apart the log corners and torn up two sides of mesh.

"Who would trash our raft?" I cried. "We were gone, what? An hour?" I kicked a good-size rock, sending it flying into the lake.

It didn't make me feel any better. I still wanted to hit something.

Packrat's face was bright red and his hands were clenched in the pockets of his coat. If he were a cartoon, there'd be steam coming out of his ears. He hadn't even been this mad when Roy had a finger on his chest. "All that time we spent on it!" he muttered. "Good thing we weren't gone any longer, or they might have totally taken it apart."

I didn't think of that! Whipping around, I looked down the beach. There were a few little kids wading in the swimming area. None of them could have dragged it two inches, never mind taken it apart. All their parents either had a nose in a book or were listening to music with their eyes closed.

I thought my head was going to explode. "I should have put it on the golf cart."

"I could have made you, but nooooooo. All I could think about were those grilled cheese sandwiches."

We jogged to the other side of the beach, stopping to ask the adults if they'd seen anything. They hadn't. And they weren't regular campers, so they couldn't tell us whose boats had come and gone.

Standing on the dock, I said, "Mr. Beakman's boat is out."

"Roy's boat is in." Packrat crossed his arms. "Roy could have been on the water, seen us drag the raft into the bushes, and come in off the lake to trash it."

I pointed down at the dock we were standing on. "Mr. Beakman could have stood here, seen us stash it, then trashed it and gone out on the lake."

As we walked back toward the broken raft, Packrat froze and put out a hand to stop me. "Hey, look. A footprint." We put our feet up against it and looked down.

I shook my head. "Two sizes bigger—maybe more. Mr. Beakman?"

"Roy?" Packrat suggested. "He's a pretty big kid."

Suddenly, a third boot stepped up next to ours. A bigger boot. The exact same size as the footprint.

Packrat and I jumped back.

Tom laughed at us. "Looks like my boot is just the right size. You guys aren't looking for Cinderella, are you?"

Tom had his humongous camera on his shoulder, the one he used when he was taping something interesting for his TV show.

"Someone wrecked our raft," I said.

"The loon raft?" Tom looked until he saw what I was talking about. "What the—?" He shook his head sadly. "Wow. I'm sorry, Cooper. I heard what you were trying to do for the loons, and I stopped by to ask if I could interview you. Who'd want to wreck your loon raft?"

"The same evil jerk who put the board in the dam."

Tom lowered his camera. "What makes you think that?"

"It has to be the same person. Whoever it is wants to get rid of the loons."

"Cooper, I'm not sure—"

Woou-ou-ou-ou.

A loon's haunting wail reminded me of why we were here. I looked out over the lake and groaned. Running a hand through my hair, I said, "We don't have time to figure out who did it now. Packrat, you're going home tonight. I have school tomorrow, and chores, and I can't go out on the lake alone anyway. If we wait till next weekend, the loons might pick another spot. A bad spot."

Packrat practically had his nose on the camera lens. "That thing isn't on, is it?"

Tom laughed. "Not yet. But I really would like to tape the two of you building your raft."

"Okay with me. But first," Packrat pulled a notebook and pencil from his pocket, "I'm going to sketch this footprint."

We rebuilt, starting with re-nailing the corners, then fixing the mesh. Pulling the mesh tight before re-stapling it onto the logs was harder this time, because it was all bent up. We ran our gloved hands over all the edges to make sure we hadn't left any sharp points.

Finally, it was time to float it in knee-deep water, mesh side down. I grabbed the two lengths of rope, tossing one to Packrat. As we unrolled them to tie them in opposite corners, we noticed that one was a lot shorter than the other. "Doesn't matter," I said, as we tied half a cement block on the other end of both ropes, "we've just gotta make sure they aren't too tight when we drop these anchors."

With our gloved hands, we made a layer of decayed wood, dead leaves, pine needles, and downed twigs on top of the mesh. We added chunks of mud with roots running through it on top of that. Then we put in some dirt until the log frame sank a little way into the water.

Tom asked questions as we worked. When I answered, I tried hard not to look into the camera. Packrat didn't care, though; he kept talking like Tom was holding a shovel instead of a camera.

Next, we dug up cattails, mosses, and ferns from the edge of the lake and planted them on three of the four sides. This would help keep the wind and any waves it made from splashing up into the nest. We left one end open, thinking that's where the loons could climb on to build their nest. In the middle, we threw tiny twigs, grasses, leaves, reeds, and other stuff I'd seen on the loons' nests before.

I went to get the red canoe off the dock, and paddled it over. Packrat set the cement blocks on the canoe floor, then gazed back at our raft. "If I were a loon, I'd nest on it."

I laughed. "Let's hope they like it as much as you do."

"If we put it in the perfect spot, I think we've got a good shot at it."

Tom lowered his camera. "Thanks, guys! I'm going to take a few minutes of tape of you paddling away, towing the raft behind you, then I'll drive home. After you're done, I'll go out and get some footage of the raft in place." He held up a hand. "I promise to stay two hundred feet away, or more. Stop by my place on your way back, okay? I might have some follow-up questions."

Packrat waved to Tom as we paddled out, but I was lost in thought, thinking about where we should put it.

"Let's anchor it behind the left side of Ant Island. That's close to where they nested last time. It'll be kind of hidden, too, because most of the boaters stay on this side of the island where the water's deeper. And the island will also block most of the waves from boaters."

While I'd been talking, the hum of a motor had been getting louder and louder.

"It's Mr. Beakman," I said, under my breath.

When he saw us, Mr. Beakman started to raise his hand to say hi. Then his eyes darted from us to the raft we were towing. His hand stopped in midair, then dropped. Eyes narrowed, he glared at us as he went by.

Packrat frowned. "Cooper, how do we know the nest won't get wrecked again? If we put it behind Ant Island, we can't check on it from the campground beach."

"We can't," I said. "But Tom will." I stopped paddling long enough to point off to the left. "That's Tom's house. If he's doing a show on the loon raft, he'll be keeping track of them."

Packrat and I paddled around the left side of Ant Island, then traveled up and down the length of it. We were sweating and breathing hard from the extra weight of the cement blocks and towing the raft. But we had to make sure it was protected, and that Tom and the people in the other two houses could see it from their docks. With all of them watching, I was hoping no one would dare mess with it.

We finally picked the perfect spot. It was about forty yards from the shoreline, where the loons' first nest was, and the water was at least six feet deep, just like the directions said.

I had turned around in the canoe to help Packrat with the anchor, but he said, "I got it." He slowly stood up, lifting one of the half-blocks by its rope.

I grabbed both sides of the canoe. "Careful."

He swung the anchor a tiny bit, just enough for it to hang out over the water. Then he let it go. The resulting splash soaked him from head to knee.

I laughed. "Is it cold?"

Packrat pulled a small hand towel from his pocket before he sat down. "Actually, it's warmer than I thought it'd be."

We placed the second anchor without any splashes. The rope on this one was the shorter one, so it didn't hang in the water as loosely as the first, but I figured between the two, the raft would have enough room to rock over waves or go up and down with the water level.

Perfect.

I gave my best loon call. "Here it is!" I yelled out over the lake as we slowly floated away from the nest. "Here's your new nesting spot!"

Chapter 15

Fishing line left floating in a lake is a danger to loons. It can get tangled in their wings and render them flightless. It can tie their bills shut, causing them to slowly starve to death.

I hoped I didn't get in trouble for not going right back to camp, but I wanted to canoe over to the three houses across the lake from the raft. I wasn't sure if they even knew what a loon raft was, or why we'd built it. I didn't want them to take it out of the lake, thinking it was floating junk. Besides, this way, I knew they'd keep an eye on it for sure.

The family at the first house didn't know the loons had lost their nest. I wanted to say, "Really? How could you not!" I mean, I'd give my right arm for a chance to watch their nest from my deck. But I did my best customer-service smile and went on to explain our idea and how our raft had been wrecked.

Mrs. Cord exclaimed, "That's terrible, Cooper! Of course we'll help you keep an eye on it."

She called to her son Brent, asking him to bring the binoculars. I showed them both where to look for the raft. I'd met Brent once or twice. He was a couple of years younger than me, but he'd just moved up from Webelos to my Boy Scout troop. An okay kid.

Mrs. Cord beamed at us. "Brent, isn't your troop working on their Bird Study Merit Badge? You know, the one with the requirement to identify twenty species of birds in their natural habitat?"

Brent rolled his eyes. "Yeah, yeah, I know. I'll keep a field notebook of what I see."

I knew what Brent meant. I liked doing the stuff for my badges, but the charts and logs were a pain.

"If you do see anything interesting, call me," I said. "Maybe Packrat and I can come over to take you out with us to see the raft a little closer. You could get some pictures, if you want."

"Sure!" Brent beamed like his mother.

The next stop was the Wentworth house. They were an old couple, in their seventies, I think. Mom said they'd lived in their house from the day they were married. It was kind of a shock to see a FOR SALE sign on their lawn.

We'd just finished tying up our canoe when the eagle swooped in from the lake, a fish in its talons. It flew to the top of a nearby red pine to sit on the edge of its nest. A chick's head poked up to grab hungrily at its supper.

"There's two in there, Cooper!" Mr. Wentworth said, as he stepped on the dock. "This is the first time in a long time we've had two survive their first month."

I waited until I'd introduced Packrat to him before blurting, "Mr. Wentworth, you're selling?"

He ran a hand through his thin gray hair. His eyes lost their twinkle as he waved that same hand toward the house. "It's too big for us now. None of our kids want it, which surprised us both no end." He shrugged his shoulders. "I'm sure a nice family will move in, Cooper. The realtor thinks it's the perfect property for someone with kids. With the water level so high, we even have a nice sandy beach again. No weeds. That'll be a great selling point."

I nodded, and looked over Mr. Wentworth's shoulder at the large white house. It would feel weird to have someone else here, but it might be nice to have a couple more kids as neighbors.

Packrat explained everything this time, starting with how the water level had risen, flooding the loon nest. Mr. Wentworth frowned and glanced at his sandy beach, but he didn't interrupt. Instead, he listened as Packrat described how we'd built the raft and anchored it. His eyes brightened when Packrat asked for his help.

"Of course we'll keep an eye on it for you," Mr. Wentworth said. "It'll be our last gift to this beautiful lake. Now show me with your binoculars where you anchored it."

Our third and last stop was Tom's house. He was waiting, ready to tie our canoe up to the dock.

"Cooper," he said, as I threw him our rope, "I saw where you put it! Great job."

He asked for my reasons and took notes. I knew he'd mention them on his show. When he was done, I asked, "Kind of sad, huh? About the Wentworths selling?"

"Yes and no, Coop. Sometimes, when you get older, caring for a big house is too much work. Not to mention putting a dock and boats in and out every spring and fall."

"Hey, Coop!" While Tom and I had been talking, Packrat had been watching the lake with his binoculars. "You've got to see this!"

"They can't be nesting already!" I grabbed the binoculars from him.

"No. But they're swimming over there. Maybe they'll check it out."

Tom lifted his binoculars. "Look at that! It's a good sign, boys. Well done."

Packrat spoke up. "You'll keep an eye on it for us? So no one wrecks it again?"

"Sure. I can do that." Tom patted his binoculars. "I'll keep you posted."

We talked to Tom for a few minutes before he made a face and said, "I just remembered—your mom called to see if I'd run into you."

"Really? I must have turned my radio down." Pulling it out of my pocket, I pushed the button and said, "Mom? You're looking for me?"

"There you are!"

I pulled the radio away from my ear and grimaced. Turning down the volume first, I answered. "Mom! You should see our raft! It's so cool. We've got it anchored and everything."

I lifted my finger up off the button and grinned at Packrat. But my grin didn't last long.

"Well, I have one very upset little girl here, Cooper. You promised she could help."

Packrat and I groaned at the same time. Tom smiled encouragingly as I looked at the radio in frustration before hitting the button. "Oh, man. I'm wicked sorry, Mom. I completely forgot! Honest! The raft got wrecked while we were at lunch and we had to rebuild it in a hurry to get it on the lake today."

"You could have finished it up tomorrow."

"How? There's school, and a bathroom cleaning." I took my finger off the button and sighed. Then I pressed it again, "Listen. Is Molly there?"

"Yes. She's here."

"Hey, Molly? I'm sorry I forgot."

"I didn't even get to see it first!" Molly whined.

"I know, I know." At least she wanted to see it. "Maybe we can get Dad to take us out to look at it this week."

"I want to go now!"

"Ask Mom or Dad."

"Daddy's still working on the roof. Mommy's stuck in the store."

"We'll talk to Dad at supper, okay? See when he can do it?"

A few sniffles. Some murmuring that sounded like Mom. A couple more sniffles. "Oh, okay," Molly mumbled.

Packrat waved my sketch of the raft in front of my face. "Oh! And you can keep the sketch I drew of it."

"Really?"

"Meet us at the store in ten minutes and it's yours."

Another Molly meltdown taken care of.

Chapter 16

Loons have a flap in their nostrils that closes when they dive. This helps keep the water out.

As we pushed off from Tom's dock, the sun was just below the treetops, and dropping fast. I had to be back in the campground by sundown, or I'd be in big trouble.

I sat in the back of the canoe, as the helmsman. Packrat sat up front. I paddled on the left, Packrat, on the right. One, two, three strokes, then we'd switch sides without either one of us saying anything to the other. I was staring over my left shoulder at the reddish clouds lining the sky, when I noticed two boats side by side in the distance. Pulling out my binoculars, I gasped. "It's Beakman and Roy!"

Packrat laid his paddle across his lap and looked back at me. "What are they doing?"

"Talking. No. Arguing. Yeah, definitely arguing. Mr. Beakman looks mad. He has a finger pointed at Roy. If he leans any closer toward him, the water's going to come over the side of his boat."

Packrat squinted toward the boaters, then pulled out his binoculars too. "Roy's arguing back. Hey! Did Mr. Beakman give something to Roy?"

I'd seen it too. "Did you catch what it was?"

"Couldn't tell, but Roy's stashing it in his tackle box. Uh-oh. They saw us."

Dropping the binoculars to our laps, we grabbed the paddles.

Packrat shuddered. "I'll tell you one thing—I don't like Mr. Beakman's face any better up close than I do from across the campfire."

91

"Stick to the shoreline," I said, hearing Roy's motor roar to life. "It's getting pretty dark, and we don't have lights."

Packrat pulled out a flashlight and held it between his knees, facing out.

I laughed. "That works."

Roy buzzed by us, not even looking our way.

Packrat and I paddled quickly, trying to beat the sunset. When we reached the dock, Roy was on his bike, tackle box in one hand and a pole in the other.

"Listen," he snapped at us, as he lifted one foot onto a pedal. "I'll only say this once: You'd better keep a close eye on that precious raft of yours. I saw where you put it. Anyone could get at it."

I met his gaze. "Tom and his neighbors are watching it for us."

Roy nodded.

Packrat yelled, "Hey! What's your boot size?"

Roy hesitated. "What's it to you?"

"Someone wrecked the raft this morning. We found a print."

"I'm a ten," he growled. "But lots of guys are size ten." Without another word, he pushed off on his bike and rode toward his campsite.

"So what was all that stuff about the raft?" Packrat said. "I mean, was he threatening us, or was he—"

"—worried about it?" I finished for him.

Suddenly the dock shifted under our feet as a familiar gravelly voice spoke behind us. "I'd say he's tired of those loons outfishing him, like everyone else around here!"

I turned so fast, Packrat had to grab my arm so I didn't step off the dock. When had Mr. Beakman come in off the lake? He had to have paddled in. What had he heard?

He pushed past us and had almost reached the end of the dock when Packrat called out, "Mr. Beak—Mr. Bakeman!"

I groaned.

Mr. Beakman stopped. He turned to spit out one word. "What?"

"What's your shoe size?"

"Ten," he said, storming off the dock to toss his fishing rod and tackle box into the back of his truck.

Packrat and I walked side by side up the dirt road toward the campground office in the very last of the day's light.

"Well, that cleared things up," I said.

"Yep," said Packrat. "As clear as the mud we caked on that loon raft."

Chapter 17

The wake from a boat can easily swamp a loon nest or overtake a newly hatched chick.

Mom and Dad did say "Good job" when I told them all about building the raft, finding the right spot for it, and how all our neighbors were going to help watch it. I really didn't feel the love, though. Dad gave me the don't-feel-bad-if-the-loons-don't-use-it speech again before he went to clean the pool area and lock it up. That meant he thought they wouldn't.

Mom said, "That's wonderful, sweetheart," between customers.

Only Molly bounced up and down, asked a million questions, and told me over and over and over again how much she wanted to go see it. Molly was a good beggar, but I wasn't risking getting grounded from the lake. She was going to have to get Mom or Dad to do it.

It was Boy Scout Brent who gave me the chance to say "I told you so" to Mom and Dad. He found me in school to report he'd seen the loons moving stuff around on the raft twice. Then he begged me to take him out like I'd promised.

Great. Now I had two of them bugging me, and I didn't even know how I was gonna get myself out on the lake. It was the Friday of Memorial Day weekend, and the campground was going to be full, full, full. There was no chance Mom or Dad could take me, so I had to wait for Packrat to get back.

I jumped off the school bus and jogged up the driveway, past the line of campers leading to our store. I hadn't even put my backpack down in the house when Mom called me on the radio, reminding me about the extra five o'clock bathroom cleaning. Then she asked about my day at school, and between *Uh-huh*s, slipped in the fact that I'd be watching Molly for the rest of the day.

"C'mon, Mom!" I said.

"Cooper, did you not just walk past that line of campers?" I heard murmuring, which meant she'd covered her radio with a hand to talk to a customer. When she came back, she said, "Molly can follow along with whatever you were going to do."

"I was going out on the lake."

More murmuring. Then, "Except going out on the lake."

I turned off the radio, groaned at the ceiling, then looked down when I felt the little brat tugging on the bottom of my T-shirt. "What do you want?" I asked.

When I saw the tears dotting the corners of Molly's eyes, I suddenly knew exactly who the real brat was.

"It's okay that you don't want me, Coop. Mom and Dad don't want me either. You can lock me up in my room, so you can go see your loons." She crossed her heart. "I won't tell."

I laughed and reached out to ruffle her hair. "Lock you up? *Lock you up?* That sounds like a great idea!" I chased her around until the tears were gone and she was squealing.

"Okay, Shrimp. Let's go see if Packrat wants to go to the game room."

Packrat's mom invited Molly and me to supper. I'm not sure what Mom and Dad ate, because Molly and I were fast asleep before they came in for the night.

It wasn't until Saturday after the trash run that I was able to sneak away to see my loons.

Big Joe slipped Packrat and me a burger to chow on as we walked to the dock. We paddled out in the canoe and anchored a good four hundred yards away from the left point of Ant Island. We didn't want to spook the loons. Through binoculars, we watched as they brought small sticks and weeds to their island, arranging them just so with their beaks. They'd even moved a plant or two from one side of the raft to the other.

"I can't believe it!" I grinned at Packrat. "They're really gonna use it! Wait until I tell the warden. And my parents."

After the craziness of the campground, with people and cars coming and going, the screen door slamming, and my radio barking orders, it was wicked quiet on the lake. The loons looked at us every now and again, but when we didn't make a move to go any closer, they kept working at their nest.

The eagle flew overhead, landing in a tree on Ant Island and staring down at the loons' new nest. I imagined it was daydreaming about eating baby loons for lunch sometime soon, and I shuddered. The loons must have been thinking the same thing, because one of them puffed out its chest and flapped its wings toward the eagle.

Aaaaa-aaa-a-aaah-aaah-ou-aaah-aaah-ou-aaah-aaah-ou.

"Whoa. That's a new call," Packrat said.

"The yodel. Only the males give it. He's letting that eagle know that this is *his* space."

The eagle stared at the loon for a little bit longer, as if to say, "You don't scare me."

The loon moved closer to the island and reared back again.

Aaaaa-aaa-a-aaah-aaah-ou-aaah-aaah-ou-aaah-aaah-ou.

The eagle lifted its beak proudly, spread its wings, and flew off.

The cool moment was lost when my radio crackled. "Coop? Almost suppertime; I need you to feed Molly for me."

I looked at Packrat. "Sorry."

He shrugged. "No big deal. I'll help."

As we turned the canoe to head for home, a boater I didn't recognize came zipping across the lake. His wake had our canoe rocking back and forth, back and forth. Luckily, Ant Island was between his wake and the raft, but it had me wondering.

"What if a boater didn't know the raft was there and he whipped around this end of the island?" I asked Packrat.

We sat for a bit, looking at the lay of the land. The raft was only a few hundred feet from this side of Ant Island. I was kind of wishing I'd put it farther away from the corner. It really blended in with the water and island shadows, which was good for hiding the loons, but bad if the boaters couldn't see it.

Packrat tipped his head to one side. "What if we marked the spot? Like people mark shallow areas."

"You mean, with floats?"

"Yeah. If we took a couple of milk jugs, painted LOON and NEST on their four sides, and floated them straight out in a line from this end of the island. People would have to take the corner wide."

I sat straight up. "That could work! We should make two of them say GO SLOW so the boats slow down, and their wake isn't so big, and the raft doesn't rock too much—

"Oh, wait." I'd just had a bad thought. "Wouldn't that be like putting up a big blinking neon sign that says SEE LOONS HERE. TAKE PICTURES AND STUFF." I sighed.

Packrat shrugged. "Then let's just do GO SLOW. They'll think it's just shallow water."

"Yeah." I smiled, thinking this might be just the thing to impress my parents. "Let's do that."

At the Sunday-night campfire, Dad told his friends, in his there-goes-my-son-playing-game-warden-again voice, how Packrat and I had put out GO SLOW signs on the lake because the loons had actually built a new nest on the raft, and wasn't that amazing?

Way to go, Dad! Tell the whole world where to find them! So I quickly told everybody how they had to give the loons lots of space, and if they saw anyone go too close, to nicely tell them to back off. I even made sure I told them how all the neighbors were watching it for us, and I said it real loud so Mr. Beakman would hear too.

That had Mom telling the whole campfire group how cute I was as a little kid, playing game warden in Deering Oaks Park back in Portland, before we'd moved here. She had this long, stupid story about how I had to count the ducks every time we went.

I was about to leave before they totally embarrassed me, when Squeaky Lady asked where Packrat and I had gotten the idea for the warning floats.

See? Even she was more interested than my parents.

I was halfway through my story when I suddenly realized Packrat wasn't sitting next to me anymore. My crazy friend was on his hands and knees outside the circle of benches, checking the soles of my father's shoes!

"Cooper?" Dad waved a hand in the air in front of my eyes.

"Oh! Sorry . . . sorry, Dad. I forgot what . . . umm . . . I was gonna say."

"I asked what you used for your water signs."

"We . . . umm . . . we found some five-gallon water jugs in the recycling bin. We . . . umm . . . spray-painted them, and umm . . . tied rope with a cement block at the other end . . ."

People kept asking questions, and I tried to keep them interested in me. I'd like to say everyone was so into my story that they didn't notice Packrat crawling around. But I think it was more because he was low to the ground, and those of us inside the circle had been staring into the bright orange glow of a roaring campfire, so it was kind of hard to see into the dark behind it.

I was so glad when Packrat came walking back into the circle and sat down beside me.

"And?" I whispered.

"I didn't find a match to the footprint."

"Beakman?"

"Had his sneakers on."

I rolled my eyes. "Did you see him, though? The more I talked about the loons, the more he looked like my sister on a time-out."

Packrat crossed his arms, slumped his shoulders, and stretched out his legs. He frowned, putting his chin on his chest. Then he sighed heavily, pulled his legs in, and shifted in his seat. Glaring down his nose, he snarled at me.

Then he pretended to fart.

I laughed. It was so Beakman! Well, except for that last part.

"Hey! Did you see me almost bump into Squeaky Lady's butt when Tom asked Mr. Beakman if he'd caught any big fish today, then winked at you? Not even your sister could have stormed away like Mr. Beakman did."

That reminded me of a promise Dad had made to Molly that morning as he'd rushed out the door.

"Did you take Molly to see our raft today?" I asked Dad.

Dad's eyes locked with mine over the campfire. He sat back and crossed his arms. "No. I didn't."

He was annoyed. Tonight, that made me annoyed right back. "She bugs me every day, Dad. Today, she wrapped her arms and legs around *my* leg and wouldn't let me leave the store! Everyone was pointing and laughing. Can't Packrat and I take her out one time without you guys? Just to get her off my back? I'll make sure she wears her life jacket. And that she sits still."

"Absolutely not."

All that could be heard were the cracks and pops of the campfire as all eyes turned our way. Packrat squirmed beside me.

Dad shifted in his seat. "If anything happened to either of you, I'd never forgive myself. When Molly learns to swim, really swim, she can go with you."

"Who's gonna teach her? Huh? You can't even find half an hour to take her out on the lake to see our raft! Packrat and I worked hard on that raft!"

"I get it, Cooper." His voice made me feel like I'd stepped in a steel trap. "I haven't spent a lot of time with her lately. Or with you. But *you* have to understand that this business is what pays our bills. It's what'll get you through college, so you can be whatever it is you decide to be."

Whatever it is I decide to be? Was he kidding me?

Dad shook his head and said a little more softly. "Listen. After tomorrow, Memorial Day, things will quiet down again. I should have more time to take her out. To take both of you out. Okay?"

"Yeah," I said.

I'll believe it when I see it.

Chapter 18

The yodel call is only given by the male. He uses it to defend his territory.

Tom's story aired that next week after the six o'clock news. He told how the lake water had risen, flooding the loon nest and drowning the eggs, without really saying how. Then he showed how Packrat and I had built the raft, and told how we'd chosen the perfect spot. He even included the part where I had warned people about the five-hundred-dollar fine for going too close and bothering the loons.

Because he also said the name of our campground and showed our big entrance sign with the hand-painted loon on it, Mom's phone started ringing off the hook, and soon, her e-mail in-box was over-flowing. I stopped counting how many times I overheard her telling customers that yes, we were the campground with the loons from the *Community Connections* show. Over the next two weeks, I was pretty glad I hadn't told Molly about Dad's promise to spend more time with us, because she would have been disappointed for sure. It was like having Memorial Day weekend over and over again.

I had breakfast with them for like half an hour before I got on the school bus in the morning. Oh, and then there was the hour at supper, when they rushed in, slapped some food together, swallowed it whole, and ran out.

Dad came in for the night between seven and eight and sat down to watch television with us. When we couldn't hear our show anymore through his snores, Molly would hug him around the neck and tell him to go to bed.

Mom came in around nine o'clock every night. She'd tuck Molly in, ask how my day went, say "Uh-huh" a few times, and then go sit at her desk to do paperwork.

So when school let out for the summer and Dad asked if I'd add another quick bathroom check to my list of chores, I said "Okay." Heck, I'd do just about anything to spend time with him these days. I'd even help him pump out the toilet tanks.

"Okay?" His eyebrows went up as he tipped back his ball cap. "Well. That was easy. I thought I'd have to bribe you or something." He grabbed my shoulder and squeezed. "No matter how hard I try to schedule it, there's no way I can vacuum the pool and do another bathroom cleaning too. Thanks, Coop. If you run into a problem, call me on the radio."

Wait? Really? Dad wasn't even going to clean the bathrooms with me? Talk about backfiring. I guess I should have held out for a bribe. It was times like these when I wished I'd never tried to save that loon family. Tom wouldn't have reported on it, business wouldn't have increased, and maybe I'd still have parents.

But then campers would stop me to ask a loon question, like I was some kind of expert or something. When they told me how great the campground was, too, and especially how clean it was, I felt proud.

Talk about being confused.

Since school was out, Packrat and his mom had finally moved in for the whole summer, along with the rest of the seasonal kids. We tricked, begged, and schemed our way onto the lake almost every day to see what the loons were doing. Sometimes, when Packrat was going over to help his grandma, and I had chores later in the day, we had to go out as early as six a.m. But he was always a good sport, even though he hated waking up at what he called a "freaky hour." Red-eyed and carrying a hot cocoa, he'd stumble down to the lake with me, mumbling all the way.

"So why come?" I'd ask.

"What? And let you have all the fun?"

I liked the early mornings. The mist hung low over the lake as the sunbeams shot through the pines to bounce on the water. There was hardly anyone on the lake at this time of the morning, except for the die-hard fishermen. Like Roy. And Mr. Beakman. Though neither of them had bothered with us since we'd put the loon raft out.

The loons had laid their second set of olive-colored eggs a little over a week ago. Boy Scout Brent had called, all excited to tell me he'd thought he'd seen them through his binoculars.

Today, Packrat and I were keeping true to our word and were taking Brent out with us on one of our loon-watching trips. Brent had brought his camera and was clicking away when suddenly, a huge raven dive-bombed the loon, who was on the nest, once, twice, three times.

Brent took the camera from his eye and cried, "No, no! What's it doing?"

The loon held fast, lying with its neck down to the ground.

The raven dive-bombed again.

I started to paddle us a little closer, thinking we might scare the raven off. Instead, the loon itself slipped off the nest.

"Paddle backwards!" I said. "Back!"

We watched, horrified, as the raven landed on the loon raft. He cawed loudly, making sure the whole lake heard his victory.

Then he looked at the eggs; even pecked at one.

"No! Shoo!" Brent called.

"Careful," I whispered, even though a scream was stuck in my throat, trying to get out. "We can't scare the loon away too."

All of a sudden, the male loon popped up out of the water. It laid low over the surface, wings outstretched, beak straight out, racing across the top of the water toward its nest. Then it reared back, waving its wings.

Aaaaa-aaa-a-aaah-aaah-ou-aaah-aaah-ou-aaah-aaah-ou.

The raven flew away, scared by the quick charge and the loon's battle cry.

The loon calmly swam back, taking the two steps needed to climb back on its nest. Swaying left and right a couple times, it settled itself back on the eggs like nothing had happened.

We all breathed a sigh of relief.

"The loon showed that raven who's boss," Brent said. He lifted the camera to his eye, then lowered it again with an "Oh, man!"

"What? What's wrong?" I asked, looking around to see if the raven had come back.

Brent slapped his forehead. "I didn't get one picture of that whole thing!"

Packrat and I had taken Brent home and were paddling back to the campground. We'd been sticking close to shore, looking for turtles, when Packrat stopped paddling. Turning back to me, he put a finger to his lips and then pointed toward shore.

It was Roy. And he was trying to pull the board from the dam! Did his little meeting with Beakman have anything to do with this? Or had Roy put the board in to begin with?

I dug my paddle into the water to get closer, thinking I could stop him. But I changed my mind. "No way am I giving him a chance to strand us again," I whispered to Packrat. We pulled our paddles up out of the water.

I yelled over to Roy, "Taking out the evidence?"

He jumped, then he waved his arms in circling motions to regain his balance on the wall.

"What are you talking about?" he snarled.

"Trying to get the board out before someone figures out that you're the one who put it there?"

He stood taller. "You're nuts! I didn't put this here. I'm taking it out, though."

"So Mr. Beakman paid you to take it out?"

Roy's face got red. His mouth opened and closed several times. Finally, he said, "You've got it all wrong, Nature Boy. You always have. What do you care anyway? You've got your raft out there now for your stupid loons."

"No thanks to you!" Packrat shouted.

Roy growled. "Why don't you just say it?"

"You wrecked the frame of our raft—tore it apart," I said. "But we—"

"You're both liars!" Roy shouted. All this time, Roy had been walking down the shoreline toward us. Now he stomped forward even though it put him in the lake up to his knees. He raised a fist, saying, "I bet you wouldn't come over here and say that!"

Packrat looked at me. I looked at him.

"Come on!" Roy said. "Say it *over here!*"

Packrat whispered, "He could be lying. You caught him covering up his tracks. Now he's afraid you'll rat on him."

I nodded. It was also possible that Mr. Beakman had paid him to take care of *his* tracks. But then again . . .

"Whatever!" I said. "But you can't touch the board now. The game warden wants us to leave it there. The other wildlife has nested with the lake like it is now."

"Fine." Roy sloshed over to his boat and climbed in. Without looking at us, he pulled his motor cord and roared over to the other side of the lake.

Neither one of us said a word as we silently paddled back to our dock. I don't know about Packrat, but I thought Roy was acting awfully weird lately.

Chapter 19

Both the male and female loon work hard to build their nest.

A few days later, Packrat got to see how the loon parents trade places sitting on the nest. The one on the nest wailed, almost like it was saying, "Hey, I'm starving. Your turn to watch the little guys."

Right away, the mate who was out on the lake replied *wooo-OOOOO-oooo-ooo.* Kind of like, "All right, all right, I'm coming." After a couple of minutes, the mate on the lake surfaced silently a few hundred feet from the right side of the nest. He reminded me of a submarine, the way he could keep most of his body submerged, with only his head, beak, and the very top of his back out of the water. He looked around, hooted softly, then dived.

The nesting loon raised herself back onto her webbed feet until her entire white chest showed. Using the side of her very long, very sharp beak, she turned each egg. How did she do that without poking a hole through one of them?

She moved a stick from one side of the nest to the other, then moved a piece of grass, too, before gently settling down on the eggs.

On the left side of the nest, the loon on the water surfaced again. When he hooted this time, the nesting loon stretched her neck straight out toward the water and slipped in. She stretched her wings and shook them as if checking to make sure they still worked after sitting still for so long. She dived. She waggled a foot. She stretched her neck until the back of her head rested on her back.

Meanwhile, the loon on the water slowly and carefully drifted up to the nest. He hung there for a while, looking from side to side, until he awkwardly climbed up next to the nest. After moving a piece of grass here and a stick over there, he settled on the eggs.

I smiled, wondering how many times one loon would move the stick, only to have the other loon move it back.

Before diving away, the loon in the water hooted softly again. Pack-rat said it meant, "Watch out for ravens," which had us cracking up so loudly, the nesting loon laid its head flat on the ground.

I thought how cool it was that neither loon would leave the eggs alone. Keeping them close by, safe and protected, was their main job right now.

I only wished my parents put in half the time the loons did.

"Coop?" My camp radio crackled with Mom's voice. She was calling me from the office. "Brent's on the phone for you. He's holding on line one."

I was in the house, watching the weather like a hawk watches its prey. A humongous storm had rolled in last night. The weatherman on Tom's news station was predicting forty-five-mile-an-hour winds and six inches of rain in the next twenty-four hours.

I picked up the house phone and pressed the button for line one. "Hey," I said. "What's up?"

"Cooper? The loons are in trouble!" Brent said. "I can see the nest with my binoculars—well, kind of see it through the rain—and one end is falling down, and one loon is still on it, but I think the other one is kind of nervous and—"

"Whoa!" I closed my eyes and hoped I hadn't heard what I just thought I'd heard in his babbling. Maybe he was just exaggerating. Pacing around the kitchen, I said, "Take a deep breath, and look through the binoculars. What do you see? And talk slow!"

I actually heard Brent take a deep breath. "Soooooo, one end . . . of the loon raft . . . looks like it's . . ."

I gritted my teeth, wishing I could go through the phone line and rip those binoculars out of his hand and look myself.

". . . falling into the water."

"Falling?" I said. "What do you mean, falling? Like it broke off?"

"No. Not broke, but one corner is . . ." He paused, and I heard Brent's mom in the background, helping him. "One corner is pulled down into the water. The whole thing is tipping. Cooper? I'm afraid the eggs will roll off."

I told him to stay there and I'd get back to him.

Tipping?

Canoe keys between my teeth, I put on my raincoat, grabbed some supplies, and snuck out the back door of the house. I didn't want Mom seeing me leave from her office window. If she did, one of three things would happen. One, she'd ask me to clean a bathroom. Two, she'd ask me to take Molly off her hands for a while. Or three, using her mom radar, she'd figure out I was headed out on the lake.

As I jogged to Packrat's the back way through the woods, I went over all the parts of our loon raft in my mind. Square frame, wire mesh, dirt and moss and lake plants and anchor—

Anchor ropes. One had been long enough, but the other one was shorter. It hadn't seemed a lot shorter at the time but now, I wasn't so sure . . . Was it only a foot shorter? Or had it been more like three feet? Five?

The water level was rising. The rope wasn't long enough. It was pulling that corner of the raft underwater.

I ran faster. I'd been in such a hurry to get it out on the lake that day, I'd messed up. I had to fix this, and fast.

Packrat's mom was out, taking his grandma to the doctor's office for a checkup, so it was even easier for him to sneak out.

If we had to be out on the lake in the pouring rain, at least it was a warm rain. And the wind had mostly died down by the time we got out on the dock. Every now and again you could actually watch a strong gust move down the lake by the way it pushed the top of the water along ahead of it.

Everything about the lake was dark gray today. The water, the sky, the land. Even the leaves on the trees were a gray-green. We bailed the sturdiest boat we had, a flat-back, wide-body, gray fishing canoe. Blending in was part of my plan.

Packrat had to yell a little so I could hear him over the rain that was pounding down on the boats and the dock. "Aren't you worried they'll leave the nest?"

That *was* my biggest worry. "Can you think of another way to fix it without getting close?" When he shook his head, I added, "I just have to be fast."

"The storm's supposed to be done by two. Can't we just wait it out? Won't the water go back down?"

We stepped into the canoe, Packrat taking the back seat. I took the front. I looked up at the sky, blinking as the warm rain hit my face and rolled down my neck. "All this water has to go somewhere. The lake will keep rising even after it stops—especially now, with that stupid board in the dam. If we don't do this, the raft will tip more. The eggs might roll off. Or the loons will abandon it. Or another rainstorm will wash the nest off the raft."

I clenched my paddle tightly, dipping it in the water harder than I needed to, to push us off the dock. "We've got to give them ten more days."

We pulled the canoe up onto the shore on Ant Island, and walked across to the loons' side. Brent hadn't exaggerated. The corner I'd tied the short rope to was tipped downward into the water. The opposite corner was lifting a little bit out of the water. One adult was in the water nearby. The second adult sat on the nest, its neck stretched out flat across it.

She knew we were here.

I silently willed her to understand that I didn't mean her any harm. I knew she was nervous; I was nervous too. But I didn't have a choice.

While Packrat dug in his pockets for what I'd need, I took off my raincoat and sneakers. The back of my bathing suit was already soaked from sitting on the canoe bench. I rechecked the waistband on Dad's brand-new, super-cool, inflatable life vest. It was snug, and the belt was secure. I didn't plan on inflating it unless I had to, so I could stay as low in the water as possible.

Snap. I looked down at my side. Packrat had pulled a heavy-duty carabiner clip from one of his pockets and clipped it on the waistband of the life jacket, tying a nylon rope to that. "If something goes wrong, I can haul you in," he explained.

"I'm a strong swimmer," I said. "I have the vest, and you have my back." I wasn't worried about me.

"No, I mean with the loon. Those bills are scary." He shuddered as he handed me a second rope.

Great. I hadn't really thought of getting stabbed.

I waded into the water slowly, keeping one eye on the loon at all times. She was going to bail off the nest. I couldn't help that. But I was hoping she wouldn't scramble away in a panic and kick an egg off the raft.

No sudden moves, I kept telling myself over and over, even though I wanted to rush through the forty yards of lake to fix my stupid mistake. When the water came up to my waist, I sank down until it reached my chin, keeping only my head above water. I looked back at Packrat. He sat in the water, playing out the other end of the nylon rope as I hand-paddled my way out to the loon raft. I bet he thought sitting was less threatening to the loons than standing.

Everything looked a little different from a loon's view. The trees and the shoreline swayed uncontrollably. Good thing I didn't get seasick. The rain was really stinging my face.

I was halfway there now. I studied the nesting loon. She studied me, with her neck still flat across the nest. Then, all of a sudden, without warning, she slid forward and disappeared into the water.

I needed to move faster. I leaned forward to paddle my hands and kick my feet more quickly. Still, I kept the water up around my mouth. Reaching the raft, I tucked the extra rope in my waistband so I could use both hands to untie the knot on the tipped-down corner.

I only took the time to glance once, quickly, at the nest. There were still two eggs. So far, so good.

Kicking my feet to stay afloat, and shaking my wet hair to keep it out of my eyes, I grabbed hold of the knot to undo it. I hadn't counted on the rope being swollen. I tried pushing the rope end back through the knot. I was breathing a little faster now, partly from trying to stay afloat and partly from frustration.

No sudden moves. As much as I wanted to grab the raft edge with one hand for support, I couldn't. If I tipped it too much one way or the other, the eggs might roll off. If I tugged the rope too hard, the same thing might happen.

After wiggling, squeezing, and then wiggling the knot some more, it finally gave. I tucked that end of the rope in between my knees so I could quickly tie a new section of rope to the raft corner before it blew away from me in the wind. Suddenly I wished I'd had Packrat come out too. I was running out of hands.

Something brushed up against my right leg. Without thinking I pulled my legs away from it, dropping the old anchor rope. Luckily it didn't sink like a brick and I managed to grab it again.

For the first time, I looked up and around me. One of the loons sat on the surface about one hundred feet away. He stared me down, then dived in my direction. I shivered, and it wasn't from the cold.

Nearby, his mate surfaced, only to dive toward me too.

My hands shook as I then tried to tie the new piece of rope to the old anchor rope. I felt one of the loons pass by my feet without touching me. Then a soft bump on my thigh. They were dive-bombing me! If they used their beaks on my legs, I'd have a lot of explaining to do to Mom after this.

There! The double fisherman's knot was done. I pulled on both ends. It was good and tight. The eggs were still nestled in the nest as if nothing had happened. With a sigh of relief I turned right to swim back to shore.

There, right in front of me, was a loon. I sucked back that sigh of relief, taking some water in with it. My eyes watered from trying not to cough. Except for my hands and feet, which were paddling the water with slow circles to keep me afloat, I stayed as still as possible.

The loon looked huge—especially its bill. Way bigger than it looks when I'm watching from the kayak.

"I'm done," I whispered. "You can get back on." I floated backward, away from the raft and the loon, to give them both lots of space. Which put me farther from shore. I saw Packrat standing, looking my way with a what-the-heck-is-going-on look. I raised one hand to show that I was okay, while keeping the other on the inflation cord on my life jacket.

The loon dived under the raft, surfacing by his mate on the other side. This gave me a clear path to swim to shore. As I slowly walked out of the water, I realized the loons hadn't made a sound the entire time.

I shook the water out of my hair. The rain didn't feel so warm anymore. Goose bumps were forming on my goose bumps. Packrat tossed my raincoat to me, then unclipped the carabiner from my life jacket. He coiled the rope with one eye on the loon raft.

"Want to stay to make sure one of them gets back on the nest?" he asked.

"No. As long as we're here, they won't settle down. Let's call Brent from home."

The rain had dropped to a drizzle. We crossed back over the island to our canoe, slipped it into the water, and climbed in. We'd only paddled a couple of strokes when Packrat said, "Hey, isn't that Brent waving his arms over there?" Packrat was looking toward Brent's dock with his binoculars. "His mom's there too. Umm . . . watching me watching them. It looks like he's saying sorry, and he's pointing toward our beach." Packrat swung around toward the campground dock. "Uh-oh."

"My mom?" I guessed.

"And mine."

"They look mad?"

"I'd say. Arms are crossed. Holding umbrellas tightly. Narrowed eyes. No talking."

Strangely, I wasn't worried. I still felt too good from having fixed the raft. "What do you figure? One day of ground-ation? Three? A week?"

"They'll go for more, but I bet we can talk them down to three."

I looked back to find him grinning with me.

Together we said, "It was worth it."

Chapter 20

Loons wail to call out to family members when they feel threatened. The more eager the call, the more eager the loon is to find their family member.

The day before the Fourth of July, I convinced Packrat to meet me for one of our early-morning canoe trips. The campground was over-full, and I knew darn well Mom and Dad would be begging me to babysit Molly. Sneaking out onto the lake during the day would be impossible.

I'd already knocked on the back door of the Snack Shack and chatted with Big Joe while he whipped up two cocoas and toasted one bagel. Still, Packrat was late. Which was normal for him. But I really, really wanted to get out there. The loon eggs were going to hatch any day now.

I had one finger on my radio to call him, when a blur of pink flew at me, throwing herself at my legs and almost knocking me back on my butt.

"Coop! Coop!" Molly's shriek cut through the quiet campground.

"Shhhhhhh!" I said, squishing the urge to put my hand over her mouth. "You'll wake the place up. What's wrong?"

"I want to come, too. I won't tell Daddy. Please take me. Please!"

I shook my head. "Molly, I can't. You know I can't. They'll ground me. Then who'll look after the loons?"

"Pleeeeeeeease? Cooper, please?"

I could see Packrat slowly coming toward me. His hair was standing straight up on end, and his coat was all rumpled, the collar tucked inside.

Taking one of the cocoas from me, he raised an eyebrow. I peeled Molly's arms off my legs. "No. Go home. Now. And stay there."

When tears fell from her eyes again, I said more gently, "Have some of that Crispy Chocolate Flakes cereal stuff, and put on your cartoons, okay? I'll come back a little early to sit and watch with you."

Molly looked at Packrat as she wiped her nose with the back of her hand. "You, too?"

"You bet," he said.

I watched her go, shaking my head, waving her on every time she looked back at me to see if I'd changed my mind. When she'd gone through the front door into the house, I turned toward the lake, with Packrat right beside me.

"Dad and Mom still haven't found time to take her out," I explained.

"Poor kid," Packrat mumbled over his cocoa.

"Mom's gotta stick by the office and phone, but you'd think Dad could take her out at lunch, or after supper or something."

"He still hasn't seen our raft?"

"Nooooo. Your mom got out there with us! Squeaky Lady and her husband asked me to take them out. Big Joe, Tom, Roy's parents, and a couple I didn't even know asked us to show it to them. If the loons are bringing in all this extra business, don't you think Mom and Dad would want to check it out too?"

Down at the dock, we noticed Roy's and Beakman's boats were already out. Climbing in the canoe, we paddled out to our usual watching spot, just left of the island.

Once we'd anchored, Packrat sipped his hot cocoa and I unwrapped my bagel. I think Packrat was still dozing on and off, but I was keeping an eye on the lake.

There didn't seem to be too much going on at the loon raft. One of the adults sat on the nest, looking around. The other fished off the far

end of the island from us. Every now and then one would softly hoot to the other.

I was a little disappointed to see that the eggs hadn't hatched yet. I wondered when Packrat and I could get out to check on them again during the weekend.

The gray morning started to brighten. The sun was trying to push its way through the trees as it rose. The water looked like one large plate of glass, perfectly mirroring the trees around its edge and the marshmallow-like clouds floating up above. Dragonflies danced up and down the canoe, and mosquitoes nipped at my ears.

A big bass jumped, leaving rolling ripples on top of the water, and I thought how Roy and Mr. Beakman were missing out by not fishing this side of the lake. Sometimes I wondered if they stayed as far away from the raft and dam as possible, so no one would connect them with the scene of the crimes.

Over at the Wentworths', a couple of lights went on. I could see Mrs. Wentworth moving around through her kitchen window. Eventually, Mr. Wentworth came out on the porch with what looked like a coffee mug in his hand.

"Cooper?" Mom's voice jumped from the radio, and I jumped with it, juggling my bagel back and forth in my hands before dropping it in the lake. I sighed. It was fish food now.

"Cooper! Please answer me!"

"Mom? Geez! You scared me!"

"Cooper! Is Molly with you?"

Chapter 21

Loons dive with their wings tight against their body. Their legs and webbed feet help push and steer them through the water.

"Cooper?" Mom pleaded through the radio. "Answer me. Molly's with you, right?"

Packrat and I looked at each other. My finger shook as I pressed the radio button. "N-n-no, Mom. I saw her right before we left, but I sent her back inside. I *watched* her go inside."

"She's not in her room. Dad and I searched the whole house. She isn't anywhere!"

My mind was racing. "She's probably hiding. Under the climber? She was wicked mad at me this morning, so I bet she went there to pout."

"Okay." I heard her take a deep breath. "I'll send Dad to check. Cooper?" Mom sounded really frazzled. "Come in off the lake. For me?"

"Coming."

Packrat had already dropped his mug in the bottom of the canoe and begun paddling. I put my head down and took long full strokes without saying a word. The more water I pushed, the more nervous I got.

We were halfway back when Packrat paused, his paddle half in, half out of the water.

"Cooper?" He pointed the paddle handle toward our beach. "The dock. In the water by the dock?"

I grabbed my binoculars. I could barely see out of them. My whole body shook from what I didn't want to see, but knew I was going to.

At the end of the dock, two little hands sticking out of soaking-wet pink sleeves were hanging on for dear life. Molly was trying to keep her already-wet head out of the water.

"Paddle!" I hollered to Packrat, but he already was. Grabbing the radio, I called Mom. "Molly's at the end of the dock! Mom, *she's in the water!* Can't talk! Gotta paddle!"

I leaned forward and paddled harder than I ever had before.

"MOLLLLLLLLLLLY!" I hollered. "I'm coming! Hold on! Hold on!"

Packrat and I kept hollering encouragement to her. My arms were burning from trying to paddle, but I couldn't stop.

My chest hurt as I watched one little hand let go. She tried once, twice, to lift it high enough to grab the dock again, but she didn't seem to have enough strength.

"C'mon, Dad. C'mon!!" I willed him to pull up in the golf cart. My eyes stung, knowing I wasn't gonna make it in time. *This is all my fault!* With each stroke, another guilty thought entered my head. *I should have taken her with us.*

Suddenly, there was the roar of a motor behind me. Roy pulled up alongside and without slowing down, threw a rope to Packrat.

"I'll tow you!" he yelled.

I wasn't sure if it was the fumes or fear that made my head swim. I couldn't see past Roy and his boat. Had Molly let go? Was she hanging on? Could she hear us coming?

When we were only feet from the dock, Roy headed for the left side of it and Molly came into full view.

She was still there!

When two of her fingers slipped off the edge of the dock I stood up. As the other three let go, I dived into the water.

It was murky. Hard to see. Thank God for her pink pajamas! She was looking right at me, her hair floating softly above her head, her hands reaching for me. As I looked at her, everything seemed to be in slow motion. The last of her air bubbles rising for the surface. My strokes to her.

There were muffled sounds of people yelling above us. When I finally grabbed her under the armpits to pull her upward, time sped up again. As we reached the surface, Molly sputtered and coughed on my shoulder, her arms wrapped around my neck with a death grip.

"I got you, Molly," I whispered in her ear. "Don't let go."

I felt her shake her head "no." Her arms tightened even more. I grabbed hold of the end of the dock with one hand. Dad's face appeared above mine, Mom racing up behind him.

Dad reached out for Molly.

I pushed away from the dock.

"*I* got her," I mumbled, swimming around the dock with Molly nestled safe beside me.

When I got to where I could stand up in the water, I swung Molly up to sit on the edge of the dock and gently pried her arms from my neck. Her hair hung in soaking-wet strands, her pajamas clinging to her skin. She shivered and sniffled as I rubbed her arms.

Packrat handed me his coat. I hesitated. "But . . . but . . . that's your coat!"

"She needs it," he said, wrapping her up in it.

Molly looked even tinier in his coat, which could have wrapped around her three times. Mom got down on her knees next to us and reached out her arms. "Molly? Honey?"

Molly burst into tears and wrapped her arms around my neck again, burying her face in my wet shirt.

Mom started to cry. Dad quietly said, "Cooper, if you'd been just one minute later . . ."

I nodded over my shoulder at Roy. "He towed us in. There's no way I could have gotten here in time without him."

Roy nodded back at me. "I heard you calling her name. Looks like he did, too."

Everyone looked beyond Roy. Mr. Beakman's face was all twisted up with worry. I swear I saw tears on his face as he sat frozen in his boat, with eyes only for Molly.

Mom called out to him in a shaky voice. "She's fine. She's fine."

He smiled a little.

Molly was still crying. Big racking sobs from the bottom of her feet.

All of a sudden, as if she couldn't hold it in anymore, Mom cried out, "Why, Molly? Why? You know you aren't supposed to come down here all alone! We've talked and talked about this!"

Molly lifted her head from my shoulder. "I—I—I heard the loons call. I—I thought maybe they were close enough to see—"

Mr. Beakman yelled, "Loons! I'm sick of them causing trouble!" He started his motor and roared off, back onto the lake again.

Packrat and I exchanged what-the-heck looks.

"Did you fall off the dock?" Mom's words brought me back.

"Noooo." Molly took several deep, shuddering breaths. In a very small voice, she said, "I tried to swim." At Mom's gasp, the rest of Molly's story came out in a flood. "I was going to show Cooper so he could tell you, and you'd let him take me out to see the loons . . ."

Dad frowned. He crossed his arms and looked down at her sternly. "Molly. What have we told you about—"

"Don't yell at her!" I shouted. The storm that had been brewing inside me from the minute I'd seen Molly hanging off the end of the dock broke loose. "This is all *your* fault!" I said. I pulled Molly close.

Mom sat back on her heels, eyes wide. "*Our* fault?"

Dad frowned. "Cooper?"

"If you'd just taken her out to see my loon raft like you promised, she wouldn't have been down here. You could've done it, just to spend half an hour with Molly. You could've done it for me, to see my big project that everyone's talking about. But no—all you think about is the campground, and making sure the campers are happy.

"Well, we're both sick of you guys working all the time, aren't we, Molly?" When Molly gave me a wobbly smile and nodded, I kept going. "Big Joe and Packrat's mom have been feeding us and checking up on us. They spend more time with us than you do."

Dad said, "What are you talking about? We're doing this so we can be with you all day, every day! You can have fun, and we're just a few steps away if you need us."

I put my hands on Molly's shoulders and turned her to face them. "Does this look like she's having fun?"

Mom was crying silently, her face in her hands. But I had to get it all out; I'd been holding it in for so long.

"You're here, but you're not *here*." I punched my chest with my fist. "You're not *with* us! We don't do stuff together anymore. We don't hike or canoe—"

Dad cut me off. "You do it all the time! You were out here playing game warden this morning!"

"You still don't get it!" I yelled back, taking a step closer. "Molly and I want to do it all *together*. We want to hang out like a family again. Like we used to!"

Dad looked at me gravely. Running a hand through his hair, he said, "Cooper, I . . . well . . . we . . ."

Woou-ou-ou-ou. Woou-ou-ou-ou.

Everyone turned toward the cry. A second, louder, more urgent tremolo call sounded before the echoes of the first had faded.

Then we heard the roar of a motor.

Chapter 22

Fast-moving boats and personal watercraft are the greatest human threat to loon chicks.

"The loons are in trouble!" I jumped up on the dock, wishing I could see through Ant Island to where they were.

Packrat started to untie the canoe, but Roy yelled, "Guys, over here!"

I gently pushed Molly toward Mom. Packrat and I jumped into Roy's boat. As we started off, Dad yelled, "I'll be right behind you!"

No one said a word as Roy raced across the lake. The calls kept sounding, sometimes together, sometimes one right after another.

It stunk, having Ant Island between us and the loon raft—not knowing what was making the loons cry like that.

From the corner of my eye, I saw Tom standing on his dock, waving his arms and pointing in the direction of the raft. When I waved both arms back, to tell him we were headed there, he climbed into his own boat.

"Come on, come on, come on," I whispered into the wind.

For once, I didn't grumble about Roy's noisy motor or his speed. For the second time today, I was grateful for it.

Finally, we turned the corner and saw the raft floating.

There were no loons on it.

Packrat, Roy, and I looked around, turning back and forth in our seats and rocking the edges of the boat dangerously close to the water level.

"There!" Packrat spotted them first. Both loons were upright, dancing in the water. Mr. Beakman was bearing down on them in his motorboat.

"No!" I cried. When Mr. Beakman was within spitting distance of them, both loons dived underwater, popping up behind him seconds later.

"They're trying to draw him away from the nest. Trying to get Beakman to chase them." I stood up to wave my arms.

Beakman swung his boat around. I heard two more boats coming toward us. I hoped that seeing other adults would make him think twice. He didn't look our way, though. He only had eyes for those loons.

Once again the loons danced frantically as Beakman headed straight for them. They dived under his boat again, coming up even farther from the nest.

Mr. Beakman turned around and killed his motor, letting his boat come to a crawl. He looked at the loons, then at us. Had he changed his mind?

All of a sudden, I realized Mr. Beakman wasn't looking at us. He was staring past us. At the loon raft. He had a crazy grin on his face.

"No!" I cried above the roar of our motor. "The raft! He's going to ram it!"

When Mr. Beakman gunned his motor, I cupped my hands around my mouth and started to scream. "Stop! Get away from them, you jerk!"

I heard Dad behind me, yelling, "Cooper! Sit down!"

The wake from Mr. Beakman's earlier charge at the loons slapped our boat. Thrown off balance, I bent my knees and put a hand out to steady myself.

But my hand met only thin air, and I kept falling.

I heard Roy and Packrat yell. Dad called, "Cooper!" Then my head hit the water, and all I heard was the muffled hum of motors above me.

Kicking my legs, I pushed myself to the surface and shook my wet bangs from my eyes. The first thing I looked for was the loon nest. Then I threw one arm out over my head and swam straight for it.

He'll have to go through me to get to those eggs.

A motor revved behind me. I looked back quickly. Dad was giving Roy a stop signal with his hand. Roy looked like he was protesting.

Dad's worried eyes locked with mine. I couldn't hear him, but I could read his lips. "Come back here!"

Packrat suddenly stood, pointing and talking fast. Roy, Tom, and Dad barked something at him which had him sitting down even faster. Still, he leaned forward, pointing and talking to Roy. Roy quickly looked my way again and started shouting.

Had they lost sight of me? I waved my arms to show them where I was. When Dad stood up and started screaming at me, too, I realized something else was wrong.

Then I heard it. The roar of a motor close by.

Too close.

I turned and froze. Mr. Beakman's boat!

I dived.

I saw stars.

Everything went black.

Chapter 23

When not on the nest, loons sleep floating on deep water, away from land, to be safe from their enemies.

Bzzzzzzzzzzzzz.

That buzzing was driving me crazy. It started low and got louder and louder. I raised a hand to swat it away.

"Hey!" I heard Packrat's voice, as if from far away. "He's moving!"

I started to open my eyes, but the light sent waves of pain crashing to the back of my brain. I shut my eyes tight again. When the pain was only a dull ache, I peeked through my left eye. When it didn't feel as if someone was poking a needle through it, I opened it all the way. Then I tried my right eye.

"Whoa," I heard Roy say. "I thought he was a goner."

I swear there were ten faces swirling in front of me. No bodies. Just faces. The swirls got smaller and smaller until they fell together into only five: Dad, Tom, Packrat, Roy, and Mr. Beakman.

I tried to get up on one elbow, but the stars came back. Dad helped me lie back down again.

"Give it a minute," Tom said gently. "You haven't broken anything. You do have a nasty cut on the side of your head, though."

I was surprised to find myself lying half in, half out of the water on Ant Island. All four boats were pulled up onshore too. Dad held a cloth to my cut. Meeting my gaze, he frowned.

"What was that stunt you pulled out there? Were you trying to outdo Molly? One heart attack a day is enough for this dad."

I laughed a little, but it hurt my head.

Tom looked confused. "Outdo Molly?"

Dad's eyes turned hard. "Molly tried to teach herself to swim today and almost drowned. Mr. Bakeman here obviously thought it was the loons' fault."

Mr. Beakman's eyes widened. "She said they called to her!"

"No," Dad said firmly. "She said she *heard* the loons. Then *she decided* to try to swim."

Mr. Beakman seemed to sag. "It looked . . . I thought . . . I just kept seeing Mia."

I think the bump on my head had me confused. "Mia? Your granddaughter?"

Mr. Beakman blinked really fast, trying to hold back tears. "Two years ago, my daughter Samantha was visiting with Mia. She'd gone to the store and left Mia with me.

"I lived on a lake a lot like this one. We had three nesting pairs of loons there, and Mia was totally in love with them. Their calls. Their colors. No matter how many times we'd go out in the boat to see them, she'd want to go more. She gave a pretty good loon call." Mr. Beakman gave a tiny smile at the memory. "Even better than yours, Cooper."

Mr. Beakman cleared his throat and continued. "Mia was coloring on the porch when the phone rang. I went into the house to answer it. When I came back, she was gone."

Mr. Beakman was hunched over so far, I couldn't see his face any-more. "We found her floating in the water at the end of the dock. But it was too late. *I* was too late." His body shuddered a couple of times. Then he wiped his tears with the back of his hand. "I realized afterward that I'd heard the loons calling while I was on the phone. They'd called her to them."

No one said a word for a couple of seconds as Mr. Beakman hung his head and sniffled. The memory of Molly's face underwater, her eyes looking right at me, had me shivering. How close we had come to going through what poor Mr. Beakman . . . Mr. Bakeman was going through.

Dad wiped one cheek with the back of his hand before laying it on the broken man's shoulder. "I'm so sorry for what you're going through. To lose one of your own . . . I don't think I could survive it . . ." Dad's voice trailed off.

Suddenly, Mr. Bakeman lifted his head. His eyes searched, and once he'd found me, he tried to get to me. Roy got in his way, so Mr. Bakeman spoke to me over his head.

"I didn't mean to hurt you, Cooper. I didn't see you. I swear it. I was looking at the loons' nest, then I heard your father yelling, so I looked at him. Only for a second!" Mr. Bakeman seemed to get smaller somehow. He mumbled. "Then I felt a thud under my feet."

"Packrat jumped in to fish you out," Dad said to me.

Roy smiled. "He didn't think twice. Good thing he didn't have that coat of his on. He'd have sunk to the bottom of the lake."

Packrat shook his head. "Yeah, but if I had my coat, I'd have handcuffs for Mr. Beak—Bakeman."

Dad coughed into his hand. I saw him share a smile with Tom. "I don't think he's going anywhere, Packrat. Tom called Game Warden Kate right before he left his dock, so we'll leave it to her to sort this all out. Besides, I believe Mr. Bakeman. He didn't see Cooper."

Mr. Bakeman mumbled, "Thank you for that."

I felt really bad for the guy, but I couldn't forgive so easy.

"He almost wrecked the raft! Just like he did when we were building it."

Mr. Bakeman nodded sadly. "I did do that. I thought I needed to protect Molly. I thought if I destroyed it, you'd give up on having them re-nest. I wanted them to move on and stop calling their stupid song, luring little ones to the lake.

"But once your raft was out, I talked to my daughter. She tried to help me realize that Molly and Mia were not the same person. It worked for a while, but seeing Molly on the dock—"

I sat all the way up. "And you're the one who put the board in the dam, too! You wanted to raise the water and flood the nest so the loons would leave the lake! Then you paid Roy to take the board out." I was huffing and puffing from trying to talk. My head was starting to throb.

But both Roy and Mr. Bakeman said, "*No!*"

Dad put a hand on my arm. "Easy," he murmured, as I felt him lift the cloth and check under it.

Mr. Bakeman looked me in the eye. "I didn't put that board there. And I didn't try to take it out, or pay anybody else to try."

Tom said, "Cooper——"

I grabbed Tom's arm. "Where are the loons? Is one of them on the nest? If they don't sit on them, the eggs will go cold."

Tom smiled. "Once we'd all pulled our boats up on land and quieted down, they went back. One's on the nest, and the other isn't too far from it. Listen."

Hoot. Hoot. Hooot-ooot.

"Here's the game warden, Mr. Wilder." Roy pointed off to his right.

Dad took charge. "Tom? Can you wave her in?" He motioned for Packrat to hold the cloth to my head before standing and rubbing his hands on his pants. "The warden will want to take a statement from everyone." Dad turned to Mr. Bakeman. "No matter what she decides, I'm afraid I have to ask you to pack up your camping equipment. You're out of my campground in the morning. Is that understood?" Dad counted on his fingers. "Vandalism, reckless endangerment, harming the wildlife—should I go on?"

Mr. Bakeman shook his head.

I laid back and closed my eyes. At last, the loons were out of danger.

At least for now.

Chapter 24

Loons turn their eggs for two reasons: to keep them warm and toasty on all sides, and to ensure that the developing loon chick doesn't stick to the inside of the shell.

Mom was already at the hospital emergency room, getting Molly checked out. She's usually so cool in emergencies. I think having two kids with close calls within an hour of each other—well, it made her a little weird. One minute she was poking a finger in my chest and yelling, "What on earth did you think you were doing, jumping in front of that man's boat? I taught you to use your head, but I didn't mean you could try to stop a boat with it!" Then the next minute, she was crying and squeezing me so tight, I thought I'd need one of those oxygen thingies. "My poor brave boy! Where does it hurt?"

She yelled. She cried. She yelled some more. Back and forth she went the whole time I was being examined.

It was so embarrassing!

The doctors said I didn't have a concussion. I did have to get ten stitches for the cut on my head, though. All the way home, Mom kept telling me how I was supposed to get lots of rest and to take something for my headache.

That night at the campfire, I was the campground hero. All the kids wanted to see where I got hit on the head. The moms hugged me. The dads clapped me on the back, saying, "Good job, good job."

Roy came up to the campfire and dropped onto the bench beside Packrat and me. He scuffed his feet in the dirt, kicking out a little at a time until he had a hole going. Finally he said, "How you doing?"

"Okay. Thanks to you."

"And Molly?"

"She's good, too. Grounded for life, but good."

"Ever find out who put the board in the dam?"

"No."

Roy looked me in the eye. "Wasn't me."

"I know."

"No one paid me to try to take it out either."

I squirmed in my seat. "Yeah. About that. Guess I was wrong . . . you know . . . when I saw you and Mr. Bakeman together." When Roy's foot stopped and he gave me a blank stare, I said. "The day you two were out in your boats and he gave you something? I thought he was paying you to take out the board for him."

Roy shot me his own what-the-heck look. "He was yelling at me. I wasn't paying attention, and we kind of floated too close to each other. I ended up catching his hat with my hook." Roy grinned at the memory. "You guys would have fallen out of your boats laughing. Anyway, he was passing back my lure and giving me a three-day-long speech about being more careful next time."

"Oh."

There was a moment of silence. Then I heard him say quietly, "I was trying to take the board out because I wanted to help you and Packrat. You didn't rat us out about the bat hunting, so I thought maybe I was wrong about you. Then you started doing cool stuff with the raft and the floats. But every time I tried to help or hang out, things got messed up."

He went back to kicking dirt, and I thought Roy was maybe done talking, until he said, "There's supposed to be a big storm tomorrow.

Lots of rain again." He looked at me. "Need me to check on your loons for you? You know, 'cause you're hurt and all?"

I almost put my fingers in my ears and shook them. How hard did I get hit in the head anyway? "Umm, actually, I'll be okay to go out on the lake," I said.

"Yeah. Sure." Roy looked down at his boots again.

I looked over at Packrat. He smiled and nodded toward Roy.

"Roy?" I know my voice cracked a little, but I never thought in a million years I'd be asking what I was about to ask. "You want to come out with us tomorrow? To check on the loons, I mean? I don't think I can paddle all that way. And . . . umm . . . it wouldn't be fair to Packrat to make him do all of it."

I wasn't sure Roy heard me at first. His foot just kept going. Finally, he said, "We can take my boat. As long as you think your loons won't mind the motor."

"Nah," I said. "With all the motors today, they still got back on the nest. We'll be good."

Roy stood up and started to walk away, then he stopped. Turning back, he shot me a grin. "It'll be great to hang with you again, Nature Boy."

For some reason, Nature Boy didn't sound half bad when he said it that way.

Chapter 25

*Young loons stay under the watchful eye of their
parents until they are about ten to twelve weeks old,
when they are able to fish and fly on their own.*

Packrat and I made plans to camp out on the front lawn after the campfire. There was supposed to be a fantastic meteor shower, if the clouds stayed away long enough so we could see it.

Mom was having none of that, though. I tried putting on my best pout face, but she just grabbed my face in her hands and said, "Does it hurt? Where?"

I was beginning to think maybe I shouldn't have screamed at them for all this extra attention. Eventually, I gave up asking about the tent and Packrat slept in my room instead.

When I woke up to rain pounding on the roof and the wind slashing against the windows, I was glad she'd gotten her way.

My first thought was, *Man, I hope Dad doesn't make us do the trash run today.*

My second thought was, *The loons!*

I jumped out of bed and limped to the window. Even though it was eight o'clock in the morning, it looked like nine o'clock at night. Trees were bent in half by the wind. Cars driving into the campground had their wipers going full blast. People were struggling with their umbrellas as they ran toward the lit-up store from their sites. All of Mom's red, white, and blue banners along the porch were sopping wet.

It looked like hurricane weather out there.

I groaned. Had we tied down the loon raft well enough?

Would the extra knot I added hold?

What if one of the ropes broke and the raft went whipping across the lake in the wind? I should have used a whole cement block, not half of one.

What if the water level got so high that one of the ropes wasn't long enough again?

What if the loons went away to another lake, where they could nest in peace? If that happened, would people still come to camp?

What if . . . what if . . . what IF?

The rotten thoughts just kept coming.

Packrat and I sat at the kitchen counter eating breakfast while Molly giggled at cartoons in the living room. I drew circles on my plate with a cold, syrup-soaked waffle. Packrat talked about anything and everything except the weather outside.

"We haven't played pool in a while. Look what I got! You know, 'cause it's the Fourth." From a pocket, he pulled out a white cue ball that had the American flag painted on it.

I'd forgotten that today was the Fourth of July. I guess that was the end of being babied and fussed over . . . not that I really wanted things to get wicked mushy between my parents and me. Still, it'd been a nice change from being left alone all the time.

All thoughts left my head as Mom came into the kitchen wearing her pajamas with the little moose heads all over them. She slowly walked over to the coffeemaker and poured herself a cup of coffee, then turned to look at me over the rim as she took a sip. My fork halfway to my wide-open mouth, I sat frozen, staring at her.

Mom leaned over the kitchen island, and putting a finger under my chin, she pushed up gently to close my mouth.

I looked at the clock. It was nine. In the morning. I looked out the window at the store. It was open.

Mom tipped her head to one side, took another sip of coffee, and raised an eyebrow at me.

"Hey, hey, hey! How are two of my favorite guys?" Dad's voice boomed, drowning out the pouring rain for a minute. "And my favorite wife!" He pecked Mom's cheek when she stuck it out. Dad poured himself a cup of coffee.

Then he sat on a stool and leaned his elbows on the counter. "What's up?" he said, looking between Packrat, Mom, and me.

"I think your son is in shock." Mom smiled gently my way.

"Hmmm . . ." Dad put his chin in his hands. "And why do you suppose that is?"

"You're in your pajamas!" I blurted to Mom. "Who the heck is running the store?"

Mom laughed. "Packrat's mom just stepped behind the counter and took over, pushing me out, when you and Molly . . . " She made circles in the air with her hand while she blinked her eyes quickly, ". . . and all that stuff that happened yesterday. She did great. Better than great, really. So, I hired her to work this morning. I wanted to check on you and have a family meeting."

Here it was. Everything I'd said on the dock was going to come back to bite me right this minute. I decided I'd better backpedal. Fast. "Umm, about what I said. I was scared for Molly and feeling kind of, well, you didn't even try to see my raft and—"

Mom held up a hand. "You were right, Cooper. About all of it. We haven't been fair to you or Molly. You're both more important to us than any customer or any job. We kind of forgot about that when business started booming."

Molly skipped into the kitchen. She gave Mom a hug, then Dad, and even Packrat, who'd eaten all his waffles and swiped mine off my plate as he looked back and forth between us all with a huge grin. Climbing up on the fourth stool, Molly sang, "We're taking a day off. We're taking a day off!"

"Just the morning," I said, a little annoyed that she'd known about it before me.

Molly shook her head. "Nope. A whole day!"

Mom explained. "That's what the meeting's about, Cooper. Dad and I decided to arrange it so we all take one day off together, every week. We have to pick a day between Monday and Thursday."

Molly piped up. "It'll be Family Day! We have to take one day off together. No matter what. Right, Daddy?"

Mom half-scolded, half-teased Molly. "Somebody's been listening through doors again."

"But who'll clean the bathrooms?" I blurted out.

Dad stood up to refill his cup. "Business really picked up this year, thanks to yours and Packrat's loon raft, and Tom's news report on it. Word is spreading quickly. Great reviews are piling up online! So now we have the extra cash flow to hire some employees. I asked Roy if he'd like to earn a little paycheck each week. He starts today. Packrat? I'll sign you on, too, if you'd like."

Packrat grinned. "Yeah!"

Dad looked at my stitches and winced. "I want you to take today off and recuperate. Starting next week, you'll get one day off with all of us, doing whatever we vote to do for that week. You'll also get a second day off separate from us, so you can patrol the lake and keep it safe." His eyes twinkled. "But you're back to being our hardworking, do-what-ever-we-ask-of-you employee the other five days."

Who were these people, and what had they done with my parents?

"Oh, and Coop? We'll be cutting you a real paycheck for the hours you work. Half goes into an account for college or game warden school, or whatever they call it. The rest is yours. For supplies and stuff."

On second thought, maybe I'll keep them.

Chapter 26

If they are lucky enough, loons can live to be
twenty-five to thirty years old.

After our family meeting, Mom went back to work so she could train Packrat's mom. Molly raced around the house, yelling, "Monday, Monday, Monday," since that's the day we'd all voted on. She made Dad show her where it was on the calendar, so she could keep track of all our Family Days.

Dad told me to rest up. "Roy can muddle through on his own today. He says he used to see you clean the bathrooms all the time, but we should train him tomorrow so he'll be ready for Monday."

That had Molly chanting and dancing again.

"Go," Dad said to Packrat and me, as he lifted a giggling Molly onto his shoulders. "I've got her for a bit."

At the game room, I stood at the window with my elbow on the sill, chin in my hand. Packrat played pinball. Finally, a girl who was sitting on the pool table juggling the balls asked the question I'd been trying not to scream at the sky for hours.

"How long is this stupid rain gonna last, anyway?"

Packrat stepped away from his game and pulled out a handheld radio. He turned it on and everyone crowded around.

"... wind gusts up to forty-five miles an hour in some spots. One and a half to two inches of rain expected in most areas. Rain ending by late afternoon."

Everyone started talking at once. "There goes swimming," one kid said.

"We could still do it in the rain," argued another. "You're already wet."

"I was so gonna take you in basketball," said a third kid to a fourth.

"My parents wanted to hike the nature trail tomorrow; you think the path will be flooded?"

As the kids moaned and groaned and started talking over each other, Roy came running in. Throwing back his hood, he shook water off himself and onto the floor.

"Better watch that," I said.

Roy looked at me sharply. I grinned back. "Dad'll make you mop it up."

When Roy's shoulders relaxed and he smiled back, I asked, "How were the bathrooms?"

"Not bad," he said. "I'd rather clean ten boys' rooms than one girls' room, though. Do you know how much stuff they take in there? It takes them hours!"

Packrat and I laughed.

"Any word on your island—raft—whatever you call it?" he asked.

The heavy weight of the what-ifs fell on me again.

"I called Brent, but he can't see it through all the rain. Mom and Dad won't let us go out on patrol."

Roy nodded. He started talking to Packrat, while I turned away to watch the rain fall. I imagined life if the loon raft was lost, or if it tipped so the eggs fell to the bottom of the lake. The campers would all leave. Maybe they'd even be mad at me and tell all their friends not to camp here. "He's the kid who messed up the loons' nest," they'd say. "Couldn't even protect them from the rain." Then Mom and Dad would have to fire all the new help and put things back to the way they were.

Through my crazy thoughts, I heard Roy say, "Tom drove in—"

I whipped around. "Tom's here?"

Roy nodded. "He's in the store. Having coffee with your dad."

"Why didn't you say so? Maybe he's seen something!"

The three of us pulled our sweatshirt hoods up. Roy buttoned his raincoat, and we lined up under the porch facing the store.

The sky looked a little brighter than before, but the rain was still coming down as if someone had left a humongous faucet on up above.

"Okay," said Roy, "if I get there first, you two have to—"

Packrat and I took off.

Roy yelled, laughed, and chased us. I could hear his footsteps pounding behind me. I tried to dodge the puddles, but finally gave up. The whole road was one big puddle! When I felt my toes sloshing inside my socks and shoes, I knew I'd get one of Mom's famous what-on-earth-were-you-thinking looks.

I wondered if she'd forget all about it if I put a hand to my head, pretending to feel faint.

The three of us burst through the store door, laughing and tossing back our hoods. We all looked like dogs who'd just fetched a stick from the lake. I shook my head. Water flew everywhere. Packrat and Roy threw their hands in the air and hollered at me.

I heard Tom's voice in the back of the store and jogged toward it. Tom and Mom sat at one of the three tables in the coffee area. Dad leaned against a nearby counter.

"I know you're off today," Dad said to me, "but if you carried a radio, it'd be easier to get ahold of you. Tom's been looking for you."

"I forgot to take it. Sorry." I smiled at Tom.

He didn't meet my eyes.

Not a good sign.

"Cooper . . ." Tom finally looked up at me. "I have something to tell you."

"It's about the loons, isn't it?" My eyes stung, but there was no way I was crying in front of the guys. I stood tall and squared my shoulders.

"Yes." Tom wrapped his hands around his coffee cup and stared into it. "I've been trying to tell you all along. The first time, I got interrupted. After that, it was harder and harder to admit."

Huh? All along? The first time?

Tom looked at me. I finally understood what he was trying to say.

"You put the board in the dam?"

Behind me, Roy and Packrat had stopped joking and shoving each other. I glared at Tom. "You? Why?"

"Not for the reasons you think. It was the weeds. They were so thick last year that I clogged up a motor and it died. I didn't want to lose my brand-new one. So I pounded the board in the dam."

Tom leaned across the table, his eyes begging me to listen.

"Cooper? I really didn't know the lake would rise so high. I should have done more research, maybe talked to Mr. Wentworth or the warden. When you told me the eggs had drowned, well, I wanted to run back and pull the board out. But you said the warden didn't want that, and it would make a bigger mess. What if other animals had nested *after* the water had gotten so high?"

I nodded.

"I almost confessed again, that time I came by and you were building the raft. Instead, I did that news report to educate the public about loons and the dangers of playing with the water level of a lake. I even used your campground name to bring in more business." Tom sighed. "When you accused Mr. Bakeman yesterday of putting the board in, I knew I was still being a big chicken. I had to come clean so you'd know who'd really done it."

He paused, sighed, and turned his coffee cup in his hands. "I already confessed to the game warden. She's not pleased with me either."

"I . . ." What could I say? "It's all right" seemed so lame. And it *wasn't* all right. I swallowed.

"Can you forgive me for not being brave enough to tell you the truth? Are we still friends? I'd really like to keep an eye on your loons for you this summer. Maybe do a follow-up report on them?"

I wasn't sure what to say. I wasn't ready to forgive, but I was finding it hard to be mad at Tom. So I used one of Dad's tricks.

I changed the subject.

"Did you see the loon raft today?" I asked.

Tom shook his head sadly. "The rain was coming down too hard. I drove over and was detoured twice." He looked at my dad. "Lots of washouts around town, but your driveway's still okay. Makes your teeth chatter together, though."

Dad nodded. "Tom, you're welcome here anytime. People make mistakes." Dad looked at Mom, then at me, with a knowing look.

I smiled a little smile. "And you helped catch Mr. Bakeman."

Tom picked up his cowboy hat and nodded sadly at Mom. "I appreciate that."

He thanked Dad for the coffee, then turned to me and held his hand out for me to shake. "Thanks, Cooper. I owe you one. A big one. Remember to call if you need anything. Or stop by."

Tom started out, but turned when he reached the doorway.

"You, Cooper Wilder, will make a great game warden someday. Keep doing what you're doing."

Tom put on his hat and pushed it back with one finger. "By the way, did you notice that it's stopped raining?"

Chapter 27

Loon chicks ride on a parent's back to stay warm and safe from turtles, eagles, and large fish. They ask to ride by nudging up against a parent's side.

Packrat, Roy, and I ran to the lake and hurried down the dock. I was about to jump into Roy's boat when Packrat grabbed my arm and pulled me backward.

"What the—?" I said.

The water was ankle deep in the boat. I groaned. There was no time for bailing!

By the time we'd finished and climbed in, my stomach was all twisted.

What would we find out there?

Roy had the boat going as fast as he could. Packrat sat up front, while I sat on the middle bench. When Roy slowed to trolling speed and then crawled around the end of Ant Island, I leaned forward.

"Look!" I said. "The raft is still there!"

Packrat and Roy cheered.

"I can't tell if there's a loon on it, though. She might have her neck down."

Packrat dug out his binoculars. He had them halfway to his eyes when he passed them to me instead. "I can't look," he said. "You do it."

I smiled. Looked like I wasn't the only one who was a little nervous.

Roy tapped me on the shoulder. "Tell me where to go," he said.

Roy still had the boat crawling closer. When we were three hundred yards away, I had him cut the motor. Packrat threw the anchor while I held up the binoculars to my eyes and searched.

I searched again.

My heart sank. "There's nothing there." I couldn't believe what I was seeing. "No loons."

"What about the eggs?" Packrat asked.

I shook my head as I scanned the entire lake. I lowered the binoculars. "Nothing."

The three of us went quiet.

Somewhere in the distance, the eagle babies cried for their supper. A screen door slammed. The wind shook the leaves on the trees, making it sound as if it were raining all over again.

But there were no loon calls. No soft hooting. No tremolo call.

Roy fiddled with the pull rope to the motor. Packrat stared off toward Ant Island.

Me, I wanted to scream. Throw the binoculars. Stamp my feet. Pound the water.

Why? After everything we'd done? Everything we'd been through! We'd lost them all.

I handed Packrat his binoculars and he put them away. I nodded to Roy and he wrapped his hand around the pull cord to head for home.

Hoot. Hoooooot. Hooot.

Roy stopped. Packrat's head shot up and he looked at me with round eyes. I looked at Roy. He was grinning and pointing toward the other end of Ant Island.

The loons had swum around the corner and were coming toward us. As they got closer, I could see one gray baby on a parent's back. This was my favorite thing about the loons—how they let their babies hitch rides to stay warm. I'd never seen it with my own eyes before, though. Mom and Dad and Molly just had to see this!

I knew what I was voting to do on our first Family Day.

Packrat almost fell out of the boat when he spotted a second baby, swimming between the adults.

The loons drifted closer. And closer still. Roy put his hand on the pull cord to put some distance between us and them.

"No," I whispered. "They came to us. If we just stay quiet, it'll be okay."

The three of us watched as the loons swam so close, we could see the red of their eyes.

"I think they're showing off their babies, Cooper," Packrat whispered. "They're saying thanks!"

I know I sat a little taller, watching those loons hang out together as a family. We saved them: Packrat, Roy, and me.

Hoot. Hoooot. Hoot.

Without thinking, I cupped my hands around my mouth and answered with my best soft hoot call.

One of the parents stretched out its wings and flapped them twice, bill in the air. Tucking them back against its body, it then waggled a webbed foot our way before leading the family away from our boat.

"You're welcome," I whispered. "Stay safe."

Acknowledgments

Cooper and Packrat is a story near and dear to my heart. The setting is borrowed from my own beloved campground. It's written for middle schoolers, whom I teach. Most importantly, though, at its heart, this book is about family. And that's something that means more to me than anything.

Along the way, so many people of all ages have helped with *Cooper and Packrat* by critiquing, cheerleading, advising, discussing, or just plain kicking me in the butt when I needed it. I want to thank them here. If I forget anyone, please know it was by accident. I'm grateful to each and every one of you.

For twenty years now, my Poland Spring Campground campers have been a source of inspiration. Especially my awesome camping kids. They talk book-talk with me. They report in on the wildlife of Lower Range Pond. They've eagerly brought me frogs, turtles, insects, and snakes. They've saved an abandoned baby squirrel. Once, they even found the jawbone of what we think was a baby deer. If Cooper and Packrat were real, they'd hang out with all of you in a heartbeat.

A humongous thanks to Big Joe, our campground coffee-maker extraordinaire, for lending me his name after having camped with us for so many years. And to my adorable nephew, Cooper Lavallee, for loaning me his name before he was even born.

I spent countless hours, over the years, monitoring our loon pair on Lower Range Pond. I saw successful nests and flooded nests. I witnessed chicks beating all odds, and yes, I even saw a loon egg overcome by rising water. My campers kept me informed too, bringing me photos and videos. During the long, cold winter months between loon sightings, I turned to my favorite websites and blogs. There were many, but I'd be remiss if I didn't mention Maine Audubon's Maine Loon Project, New

Hampshire's Loon Preservation Committee, and Larry Backlund's Loon Blog; these were invaluable to me.

I also received endless support from the amazing students and staff at both Poland Community School and Bruce Whittier Middle School. I have the best time working with each and every one of you, especially Shannon Shanning and her students, in whose room I assistant-teach. Our trail time, read-alouds, writing-share circles, and cook-offs against the Poland Fire and Rescue staff are the highlights of my teaching weeks. I learn so very much from all of you.

All authors have a circle of writing friends to turn to in good times and need-a-hug times. I'm blessed to have so very, very many. I wish I could get you all into a giant room to give you a proper thank-you. A special shout-out goes to my Schmoozers; Cindy Lord, Carrie Jones, Val Giogas, Mona Pease, Anna Boll, Jo Knowles, Cindy Faughnan, Mary Morton Cowan, Laura Hamor, Denise Ortakales, Jeanne Bracken, Nancy Cooper, and Joyce Johnson: You helped make *Cooper and Packrat* shine.

Another huge thank-you goes to Dean Lunt and all the Islandport Press staff for their excitement over this eco-adventure, especially Melissa Kim, whose editorial guidance, faith, and patience have made this first-novel journey everything I'd hoped it would be. Thanks for loving this book as much as I do.

And Carl DiRocco . . . there are no words to adequately express how very much I treasure each and every illustration. You brought Cooper and Packrat to life right before my very eyes!

There's my ginormous family and family-in-law, too. Sisters and brothers, cousins, nieces, nephews, godsons, aunts, uncles, and cousins. Some are near, and some are far, but all have yelled from the rooftops to spread the word about *Cooper and Packrat*. Your support means the world to me.

Mom and Dad, *you* are the originators of Family Day. Our Sunday without-fail-rain-or-shine outings to Misquamicut Beach and Holland

Pond shaped my childhood and will forever hold a special place in my heart.

To my "other parents," Ron and Lee: Not many families get the opportunity to run a three-generation business. Working Poland Spring Campground side by side with you was priceless, and we have a gazillion happy memories to show for it. Reflections of them are sprinkled throughout these pages.

Alex and Ben, we've had sooooo many amazing Monday Family Days, haven't we? Hikes up Tumbledown, lying on Old Orchard Beach, kayaking the Androscoggin, visiting the Portland Head Light—even those rainy ones where we played games at the kitchen table were special. Sometimes it was only us; other times, Bryant, Nick, or Joey added to the fun. I wouldn't trade a single day for anything.

And last but not least, there's David, my loudest cheerleader, my best friend, and a firm believer in Wight Family Day. There's no one I'd rather hike, geo-cache, or kayak with. I'd happily join you on any adventure, anywhere, anytime.

About the Author

Tamra Wight lives in Poland, Maine, where she runs the Poland Spring Campground with her husband and two children. Every summer, at the campground, she meets interesting families from all over the world. During the school year, she works as a teaching assistant at Whittier Middle School. Between the two, she has more writing inspiration than she knows what to do with! She is the author of the Cooper and Packrat adventures, *Mystery on Pine Lake*, *Mystery of the Eagle's Nest*, and *Mystery of the Missing Fox*. She is also the author of the picture book, *The Three Grumpies* (illustrated by Ross Collins). When Tamra isn't writing, she enjoys wildlife watching, hiking, geocaching, kayaking, power-walking, and snowshoeing; most of these she does with her faithful lab Cookie. You can see her wildlife photos on her web site, www.tamrawight.com.

About the Artist

Carl DiRocco is a graduate of the New England School of Art & Design. He is the illustrator of the Cooper and Packrat adventures, *Mystery on Pine Lake*, *Mystery of the Eagle's Nest*, and *Mystery of the Missing Fox*, as well as *Dear Big, Mean, Ugly Monster* (a Minnesota Humanities Book Award Finalist) and *Our Principal Promised to Kiss a Pig* (a Children's Choice Selection). Carl lives in Reading, Massachusetts, and loves to camp with his wife and three sons.

The Cooper and Packrat Adventures

Mystery on Pine Lake

Trouble has come to Wilder Family Campground and Pine Lake, where a family of loons is building a nest. Cooper Wilder and his new best friend, Packrat, must figure out who is trying to harm the loons, and stop them before it's too late.

Mystery of the Eagle's Nest

When Cooper and Packrat find their geocache box full of illegal eagle parts, their lazy summer is over. Someone wants those valuable parts back. And if they can't get the parts back, they'll settle for holding one of the rare Pine Lake eaglets hostage instead.

Mystery of the Missing Fox (coming Spring 2016)

Who would kidnap a fox kit? And why? Cooper, Packrat, and Roy must protect a fox den, find the kits, and rule out Summer, the new girl who lives across the lake, as a suspect.